A MAN

To Harriet, Jotham Gaul was nothing but an irritating boor who told her she had nothing but her looks—but why should she care about his opinion when those looks had done so much for her? He wasn't the only man in the world after all . . .

A MAN TO WATCH

BY
JANE DONNELLY

MILLS & BOON LIMITED
17–19 FOLEY STREET
LONDON W1A 1DR

First published 1979
Australian copyright 1979
Philippine copyright 1979
This edition 1979

© Jane Donnelly 1979

ISBN 0 263 73142 1/22/32.

Set in Linotype Plantin 10 on 11½ pt.

Made and printed in Great Britain by
Richard Clay (The Chaucer Press), Ltd., Bungay, Suffolk

CHAPTER ONE

'SELL up?' Harriet Brookes echoed, and the man who had been Henry Brooke's accountant said,

'That was the advice I gave your father. As you can see, the firm is heavily in the red.'

Her father had never shown any sign of being worried about money, or anything else. A couple of years ago he had sold the house, a few miles from the engineering works, and stayed in an hotel near the factory when he was down here. But that was because he had always preferred his London apartment, and Harriet had her own flat in town, and the country house was rarely used.

Well, that was what her father had told her. He had drawn a generous salary himself and made her a small allowance, and she had had no idea that the family firm was on the rocks until half an hour ago when Mr Snelson had produced the books and started explaining the figures.

'I'm very sorry, very sorry indeed,' said the accountant, sounding as contrite as though it was all his fault. It wasn't, but he felt reluctant to lay the blame on Henry at the moment. 'It was bad luck,' he said. 'Changing times.' He might have added, 'Henry always had it too easy. Henry had no stomach for a fight.'

Henry would have been putting the works on the market himself within the next six months or so, if he hadn't died of a coronary, sipping an aperitif on a friend's yacht, cruising around the Adriatic.

If he had lived and sold up Henry would have been all right. The friend was a wealthy widow and Henry had always been a ladies' man. Harriet would be all right too.

With her looks she would probably marry a fortune. She
had been engaged a couple of times already, to very eli-
gible young men, so the news that she was no heiress
shouldn't be the blow to her that it might have been to a
plainer girl.

All the same, Cedric Snelson wished she had been prepared. She was taking it calmly, but it was obviously a
shock. She sat back in her chair, her smooth brow furrowed.
'I didn't know,' she said. 'I'm afraid I was never very interested in the family business.'

Neither was her father, if it came to that. When he
inherited it it was flourishing. Over the years he had continued to draw his salary, and fill his office chair, but he
was never a worker. He was a charming fellow, whom it was
impossible to dislike, elegant and with youthful good looks.
He and his daughter had made an attractive pair, because
Harriet was even lovelier than her mother had been.

Harriet hadn't been near the factory for years. She hadn't
been in this village since the house was sold. Two days
ago was the first time since then. Yesterday Henry had
been laid to rest in the family grave and Harriet was staying with the Snelsons.

She was a part-time model. Cedric Snelson's wife pointed
her out to him sometimes in the glossy magazines, and
Henry had always mentioned it when Harriet was appear-
ing in an advertisement, sometimes in photographs, occasionally on T.V. He had been proud of Harriet had Henry.
After she left boarding school they had spent a lot of time
together, not down here but doing the cosmopolitan social
round.

Yesterday's funeral had been very well attended. The
little churchyard had been crowded, with everyone shocked
by the unexpectedness of Henry Brooke s' death, while his
daughter stood between the Snelsons, wearing a plain black

velvet coat, buttoned severely high, and a wide-brimmed black hat.

She wore no make-up, but her white face in the frame of her hat was flawless, and her hair fell in a gleaming cascade over her shoulders. Those who hadn't seen her for a long time couldn't keep their eyes off her, and those who knew her well thought that Harriet was looking as spectacular as ever.

They were sorry for her, pitying her bereavement, but some of the women felt that she might have developed pink and puffy lids instead of those poignant dark shadows around her eyes. She looked heartbreaking. She always did. That was why she could be so outrageous, downright cruel at times, and get away with it.

Almost every woman envied Harriet, but that afternoon everyone was sorry for her. 'I know how close you were' was something she heard again and again, and she nodded and held back the tears that glittered in her beautiful green eyes.

She should have gone back to London with friends, who had come to the funeral and to take her back, but she was persuaded to stay a little longer with the Snelsons. Cedric Snelson felt that she should be put in the picture about the financial state of the firm before she left, and the time since her father's death had been grim for her and a few quiet days in the country could do nothing but good.

She hadn't broken down since the news was broken to her, when she had wept wildly for the best part of an hour, then dried her tears and got on with all the things she had to do.

She didn't cry during the funeral. Nor during the evening sitting with the Snelsons and some of the people who had been neighbours when she'd lived down here as a child.

She went to bed early and Mrs Snelson brought her

hot milk. Ida Snelson had been sniffling most of the day, less from grief than because she always cried at weddings and funerals. She had liked Henry Brookes well enough, but she had resented his selfishness and laziness. He shouldn't have been on that yacht. He should have been in his office, trying to keep the factory solvent.

But she knew how close Henry Brookes and his daughter had been and she wondered if she dared sit down on the bed and put her arms around Harriet.

She was old enough to be Harriet's mother, and she remembered the plain plumpish child who had sometimes been around during school holidays. She had hugged that child when Harriet's mother had died, and felt the shivering little body huddled against her. But since then the child had changed into this sophisticated and stunningly beautiful young woman who was much less approachable.

Ida stood awkwardly by the bed. 'Try to get some sleep,' she said, and wished she could think of something to say that wouldn't sound too trite. But all she could come up with was, 'Time is a great healer.'

'Yes,' said Harriet. She was sitting up in bed, the hot milk on the bedside table. As soon as Ida Snelson closed the door she got out of bed and poured the milk out of the window on to the lawn below. She hated hot milk. She had hated it ever since they had made her drink it when she was a fat child whom nobody loved.

Mrs Snelson was wrong about time healing everything. There were some things that stayed as hurtful even after years. She picked up a hairbrush from the dressing table on her way back to bed, and sat propped up with pillows, brushing her hair.

The memories were sharp tonight, and she was afraid to sleep because she was sure she would end up with nightmares. She would be a child again. Her mother would be pushing her out of the way, ashamed of her because she was fat and sandy-haired, with a stubborn sulky little face.

'Can't you do anything with her?' her father would be asking, and her mother would say, 'Like what? How would you set about making a silk purse out of a sow's ear?'

They were quiet in that memory, contemptuous but quiet. In most of the memories they were shouting at each other, because there had always been other women for him, other men for her.

'You can get out and you can take Harriet with you,' they would snarl at each other. 'Don't imagine you're landing me with Harriet!'

She was sent away to boarding school just after her fifth birthday and she was not a popular child. She was bright enough, too bright, some of the staff felt, but solitary. Quiet most of the time, although there were the rare flare-ups when it was heaven help anyone who stood in her way, when the green eyes blazed and she showed a wild and disturbing side to her nature. But on the whole she was an amenable pupil.

Her mother died the year Harriet entered senior school. She had gone into hospital for what should have been a minor operation and a fatal blood clot had formed. No one had bothered to warn Harriet that her mother was going for surgery. She certainly wouldn't have wanted Harriet turning up at visiting hours, in the private ward that was a bower of flowers where she had expected to hold court to friends and admirers.

Harriet was called into the headmistress's room and gently told that she had no mother. Then she was helped with her packing and escorted home in time for the funeral.

After the funeral her father returned her to school on the first available train. His grief was quite sincere, and completely selfish. In spite of his womanising, and her man-chasing, he had loved his beautiful wife in his fashion, and he could see no sign of her in their lumpish daughter. He was too concerned with his own feelings to bother about Harriet's.

When Harriet began to make friends and get invited to other girls' homes for school holidays that was a relief to him. He would have been surprised to know how long it was between their meetings. He rarely thought about her at all, although occasionally the realisation that she would be leaving school at eighteen crossed his mind.

He had presumed she would be going on to university, but in one of her infrequent letters she said she had changed her mind about that, so perhaps a job would have to be found for her in the firm. In those days it was making a steady profit and Henry Brookes shelved the problem until the time came when he would have to face it. All his life he had been side-stepping problems.

Because he saw so little of Harriet he didn't realise how she was changing. Belatedly she was shooting up in height. 'You can almost see her growing,' they said at school, and for a while she was nicknamed 'Beanstalk.'

She laughed at that. She had never laughed at herself before, it was the beginning of her making some friends, and every time she looked at herself in a mirror she knew this was a sort of miracle that was happening.

The dumpy shortish girl was shedding puppy fat. Her legs were becoming long, slender and shapely. Her hips were narrow and her breasts were firm and high. She was growing tall, and as the podginess left her face and the double chin dissolved, the sulky mouth became strong and beautiful, and the slanting green eyes opened wider. Hollows formed beneath her cheekbones and the nose with flaring nostrils was revealed as straight and perfect.

Her skin had always been clear, now it seemed translucent. Her ginger-pudding-coloured hair had been darkening for years. She had always worn it either plaited or pinned back, but one night in the dormitory she cut it just below shoulder length and announced that she would be wearing it loose from then on. It was a rich dark glowing red in deep waves, and several teachers tried to persuade her to go back to the old style.

She flatly refused. 'I like it like this,' she said, and because, even at St Bertold's, the day had gone when girls could be ordered to tie back their hair, Harriet Brookes continued to toss hers back, washing it two or three times a week and brush-drying it with loving care.

From then on she was generally acknowledged the best-looking girl in the school by the other girls. She was never the most popular. There was nothing cosy about Harriet, but she wasn't grumpy any more, nor quiet. Instead she was full of energy and vitality, and she didn't give a damn. For years she had been left more or less to herself. But in her last two years at school she had plenty of admirers, girls who found her dazzling, who called themselves her friends.

They were her friends. She was fond of them. It was much nicer going to their homes during the holidays than going back to her father's house. But none of them had asked her anywhere when she was plain. Their friendship was skin deep, and she would never have confided anything that mattered to them. She never really trusted anybody. What had happened to her was like winning the pools, and realising that you could get away with murder because you were rich. It was the same with beauty. If you had it you were rich but, unless you were born with it, it could never be an integral part of you. She would always remember her mother and father shrieking at each other, 'You're not landing me with Harriet!'

Now she had neither mother nor father, and the people at the funeral who had been telling her, 'I know how close you and your father were,' knew nothing of the sort.

Harriet and her father had never been close.

She had loved him, although as she got older she saw all his faults clearly enough. But he only loved her because she had grown into a late-developing knock-out.

She practically got herself expelled from school. Nothing that made headlines, but before she went home for those last Christmas holidays she had been given an ultimatum. She was to think very seriously about her future because, in the opinion of Miss Lupton the headmistress, her conduct had been unbecoming a young lady from St Bertold's.

That was a laugh. All she had done was get her photograph into a teenage paper. There wasn't a girl in the school who wouldn't have jumped at the chance. Although Harriet had been lucky it was a genuine staff magazine photographer who approached the café table she was sharing with Paula—she was staying at Paula's for half-term—and asked if she had ever done any modelling. The magazine wanted a new face, and a lithe young body, for a fashion spread, and Harriet was the most striking unknown he had seen for quite a while.

Paula had viewed the card he produced with as much suspicion as if it had proclaimed *Playboy*, but Harriet had said, 'Anything for a laugh.'

Going up in the lift Paula had mouthed behind the photographer's back, 'What if they want you to—you know —strip off?' and Harriet had mouthed back, 'Well, I've got the figure for it.'

She had no intention of stripping, and it wasn't that kind of magazine, but it was fun to shock Paula, who would go back to school with a hair-raising account of this escapade.

Paula did. All the school waited for the magazine to come out, and when it appeared Harriet was summoned to Miss Lupton's office. The photographs were good. Harriet was extremely photogenic, and she had been delighted when she'd received her advance copies, although she had shown them to no one.

She was fully clothed in every shot, wearing teenage clothes that thousands of girls would be buying, but making them look exciting and daring. That was what bothered Miss Lupton, the defiant tilt of Harriet's chin in these photographs, the swirling cloud of her hair, and the aura of sexual promise that came over so flamboyantly. She closed the magazine, that had been lying on her desk, with an expression of distaste, and said, 'I hope we're going to have no more of this nonsense.'

The art editor of the magazine had asked Harriet to look in the office during her next school holidays, which Harriet had every intention of doing. The photographic session had been fun, she had enjoyed herself and been paid for it, and she smiled sweetly at Miss Lupton and said, 'I was thinking of making a career of it. Either that or marrying a millionaire.'

'Don't be impertinent, Harriet,' said Miss Lupton, and the interview ended with Harriet being warned that any more of this kind of thing—with which Miss Lupton dropped the magazine into the wastepaper basket—and she would be leaving St Bertold's at once instead of next August. A letter would be sent to her father, putting that on record.

A fortnight later the school broke up for Christmas, and this time Harriet went home. She had had several invitations but she wanted to see her father, to explain about the magazine and ask if she could leave school. Because she was seventeen, and she wasn't going on to college and there didn't seem much point in hanging around St Bertold's for another six months.

He hadn't written to her in ages, and she never wrote home unless she had something to say, like she wouldn't be coming for the holidays. She might have shown him the magazine, again she might not, she didn't think he'd be interested, but she did expect that Miss Lupton's letter would have caused a stir.

It was over a year since she had seen her father. He had always led a very full social life, and it would never have occurred to him to change his plans to spend time with his daughter. He was spending this Christmas in his London apartment, but he had been down at the works for the past few days and the day Harriet arrived home he went out to dinner with friends.

She had eaten alone, taking a taxi from the nearest station. The housekeeper was newish and didn't know her, and served her with a bowl of hot soup, followed by cold chicken and salads; and then Harriet sat in the drawing room and waited.

Other girls' homes always felt different from hers. Hers was a beautiful home, beautifully furnished, but there had never been any welcome in it for her. She wasn't surprised her father wasn't here, although she had written telling him when she was arriving, and there was Miss Lupton's letter. Surely he would want to see her about that. But not tonight, it seemed.

When television ended she went upstairs, undressed and bathed, and washed her hair. Her bedroom never seemed to change. White and gold-trimmed furniture, pastel walls and carpet. It had never been a child's room, but she had been in here from when she was months old. She had glared into that dressing table mirror, sitting on the stool, feet swinging, legs too short to reach the floor, while someone brushed her hair hard and brought tears to her eyes, and then plaited it tightly.

The room hadn't changed and the house hadn't changed and her father hadn't changed, but oh, how she had changed! She smiled at herself, a slow teasing smile, with a flicker of dark lashes over the green green eyes. She had seen young men gulp and goggle when she smiled like that. She had been wearing school uniform on her journey down here today—not the hat, of course, but the dark green trench coat and a pair of tan leather boots, and had basked in the admiring looks. Several men had tried to chat her up, and that was in that dreary gear. Once she got into some decent clothes life would take wings.

She heard the car coming and put on her regulation St Bertold's dressing gown, dark green towelling, wrapped a towel round her head and went downstairs.

She was in the hall when her father came into the house. He had dined and wined well and he greeted her jovially, 'Hello, my dear, I thought you'd have been in bed by now. Sorry I wasn't here when you arrived—business, you know. My goodness, you have grown, haven't you?'

He knew she had been shooting up as school clothes had had to be replaced, but until he saw her standing at the bottom of the stairs, the dressing gown tied round her narrow waist, with the towel round her head exaggerating her height, he hadn't realised that she must be nearly as tall as he was himself.

'I think I'm through with growing now,' she said, and her voice seemed different, amused and confident. She looked at him steadily. 'You got a letter from Miss Lupton?'

Now might be the time to ask about leaving school, while he was in a mellow mood. 'I believe I did,' he said. He went into the drawing room and poured himself a final whisky. 'Come and sit down,' he said, like a considerate host, and Harriet sat down while he sipped a little from his glass, standing by the fireplace. 'She asked me to get in touch with her,' he recalled. 'I must do that, but I've been very busy lately, so what's it all about? Your plans for after school? Are you going to university after all?'

He hadn't cared enough to dial a phone number. He had

assumed Miss Lupton wanted to discuss Harriet's acade-
mic future, but it would have been all the same if she
had been waiting to tell him that Harriet had three months
to live. Harriet said crisply, 'I think she's going to expel
me,' and felt a sweet deep triumph in seeing her father
almost reel into the nearest chair.

'What did you say?' He couldn't believe his ears. Harriet
had never caused any trouble. She was an awkward child,
plain as plum duff, but always quiet and tractable. He
didn't even know about the childish rages that unhappiness
had caused. That was how little he had concerned himself
with her. Now he wondered what the hell Harriet could
have been up to that would make that old trout talk about
expelling her.

Harriet explained, 'I did some modelling for a magazine,' and her father's jaw sagged.

'What sort of magazine?'

'I'll show you,' she said, and went up to her bedroom
where she got the paper out of her case, then pulled the
towel off her head and brushed through her hair. It wasn't
quite dry, but the dark red wavy mass transformed her so
that when she went back into the drawing room he stared
as though she was a stranger.

'This one,' she said.

'Thank God for that!' What kind of naïve idiot did he
think she was? What sort of modelling did he think she
might have been doing? She had enjoyed scaring him. She
had to bite her lip to stop herself bursting out laughing.
She opened it at the pages that were headed, 'Glam clothes
to watch out for and a fab girl to watch.'

'This is you?' he said incredulously.

She said nothing to that. She stood with her hands in
her pockets surveying him with a look in her eyes that he
couldn't read, as he stared at the fashion feature. Then he
looked up at her.

'Good God!' he said. When he finally stopped looking up at her and down at the magazine he said hoarsely, 'This is a shaker.'

'The magazine thought they were rather good,' she said demurely.

'They are good.' It was the first praise she had ever had from him. At one time she had come top of the form regularly in exam results, but neither he nor her mother had ever said, 'Well done,' which proved it wasn't what you were but the way you looked that mattered.

Her father was smiling at her now as she explained that Miss Lupton had taken exception to one of her pupils posing for fashion stills, and that she didn't particularly want to go back to St Bertold's. 'I thought I might take up modelling. The editor asked me to get in touch, she thought they could use me again.'

He wasn't sure about that. 'There's plenty of time to decide what you're going to do,' he said. 'But if you want to leave school I don't see why you shouldn't. I'm going up to London on Tuesday. You shall come along with me and we'll see about getting you some pretty clothes.'

From that night her relationship with her father changed radically. From that night she could do no wrong. She was the stunning girl he introduced to all his friends, as 'my daughter Harriet'. He was open-handed with money; miserly with himself, selfish to the core, but he bought her gorgeous clothes and that Christmas she was the hostess in his London apartment.

Everyone admired her. Everyone was astonished that this was Henry Brookes' daughter and Harriet lapped up the compliments, and believed them because she was beautiful and that was what everyone was telling her. She knew the power she had, and that with luck it would last for the rest of her life. But in her nightmares she was always plain and everyone turned away from her.

She still had nightmares sometimes and they never changed. The night of her father's funeral she kept herself awake because it was better to lie grieving than slip back to the time when he hadn't cared whether she lived or died.

She was going to miss him. She thought of the people who had been in the little churchyard today. Some might get in touch with her when they knew she was staying here for a few days and she wasn't sure that she wanted that. She wouldn't have much in common with folk she hadn't seen for ages. London was her home, where her father's apartment was more or less as he had left it to join the yacht and his very good friend of the moment.

He had always had a very good friend, but he had never come near marrying again, and although he was not a man on whom anyone should have relied he had represented some security to Harriet. Other men had come and gone, but he had been her father, and now there was nobody who belonged to her.

She wouldn't keep on his apartment. Her own flat was all she needed, somewhere to store her things, big enough to sleep herself and a few friends, to entertain in a small intimate way.

There was the factory down here—she didn't know then that the business was running at a loss—and for a moment she regretted that the house had been sold. It might have been a comfort to have a home where you could grow old, a house that nothing could shake.

There was one like that, just a few miles away, and Nigel Joliffe who lived there had been at the funeral. She hadn't seen Nigel for a long time and when he had come across to her with his condolences that had brought memories into her mind that had choked her for the moment. Because that first Christmas she had gone with her father to a New Year's Eve party at Tudor House. When they

came back from London there had been this party and
she had been the star attraction.

She could still remember every detail of her dress, yards
of white flowing chiffon, and her father saying, 'This is my
daughter Harriet,' and looking around the Elizabethan hall
with its small minstrels gallery and thinking, 'I'd love to
live in a house like this.'

Everything had seemed possible that night. Her power
was new and heady. Nigel, in his twenties, had followed
her round like her shadow, and she had quite fancied Nigel.
She had gone out with him occasionally in the following
months, but her father was taking her around by then and
she was meeting other men. She was engaged for the first
time within a year, and after that she lost touch with Nigel.

At the funeral she asked, 'You're still living at Tudor
House?' He was, and still farming the land around it.
He'd enquired if she would be staying down here and when
she'd said, 'For a few more days,' he'd asked if he could
phone her. 'Please do,' she'd murmured.

It was the only thing she could have said, but now she
remembered that she had liked Nigel and she wondered
why he hadn't married. Mrs Snelson had filled her in with
a little local gossip during the last few days, but until then
Harriet hadn't concerned herself with anything much that
was going on down here. It wasn't her stamping ground,
her work and friends were elsewhere. Sometimes her father
had spoken about old acquaintances; he was still meeting
them. He still came down to the factory and sometimes
news reached her in other ways.

Sometimes the country set got themselves into the gossip columns. Sometimes she met ex-neighbours, but she
wasn't on close terms with anyone from around here. She
had cut loose from her early years and her father's death
could have severed her last link.

But tomorrow Nigel would phone her, and she would

meet him and go to his home. She would like to see Tudor House again. Nothing would have changed there, except that he and his mother would be how-many-years older? Harriet had been seventeen at that New Year's Eve party; she was twenty-two now.

Five years had passed in which everything had come easily to her as soon as she turned into a beauty. She had an allowance from her father, her earnings were adequate and could have been higher if she had worked harder. But why work hard when she only had to express a wish and some man would be signing a cheque for whatever it was that she wanted?'

She had friends everywhere, and men were always falling in love with her, but after a while she began to lose interest and as soon as she started looking for faults she found them, and then she started looking around for somebody new. Her current affair had reached that stage. When she went back to London she would be seeing less of Anthony, and she had a good excuse because in future she would have to spend time down here. The factory was her responsibility now.

Her father had always stayed at the same hotel, but Harriet had seen a lot of hotels, and she didn't want to make them her way of life. She might look around for a little house, if she could find something suitable near enough to the factory. Although she had never been happy in this place she should have outgrown her childhood by now.

She fell asleep making plans, and it was a blow next day to hear that the business was practically bankrupt. After lunch Mrs Snelson had brought in a tray with a full coffee pot and then left Harriet with Mr Snelson, and a pile of account books.

Harriet poured the coffee and sat listening, letting her coffee get cold while the accountant put her in the gloomy picture. The books meant very little to her, but the sales graphs with their plummeting lines were clear enough.

'I didn't know,' she said at last. 'I'm afraid I was never very interested in the business.'

It was too late to start getting interested. If there had been a viable concern she would have taken advice and learned, and pitched in with all her strength. Not just to make money but because the life she was leading had suddenly begun to seem rather aimless, and she would have welcomed the chance to tackle something new and demanding.

But it must have been ten years since she had walked through the factory gates, and the machine rooms had always been a complete mystery to her. She knew nothing. If the experts said the firm had no future she had to accept that. She did ask wistfully, 'There's no chance at all of us carrying on?' and got an emphatic,

'None,' from Mr Snelson. He wondered how much she had relied on her monthly cheque. He knew that she lived in some style and she looked an affluent young lady, in a simple dark dress that even his masculine eye recognised as exorbitantly expensive, wearing single-stone diamond ear-studs, a square-cut emerald ring and an oval watch with a diamond-studded face.

He said, 'I wish I could have told you that your father had left you a healthy business, but at least your own career is prospering. We often see you in magazines and on the television.'

Not that often, thought Harriet. You needed single-minded ambition to make the top. Modelling had been a hobby for her rather than a profession. She said airily, 'It's been fun. I've got a share in a small art gallery too.'

She had sold some jewellery just over a year ago to help finance a friend's purchase, and sometimes she served in the sales room. That was supposed to be an investment and one day it might be. She smiled, showing her perfect teeth. 'I won't starve, I promise you!'

'Of course you won't.' Nobody, he was sure, need worry about Harriet; and he reached for his cooling coffee reflecting, 'You wouldn't have been keeping the business anyway, would you?'

'If it had been breaking even I would,' she said, and smiled again at his surprise. 'I would have liked to come back here.' She sat still, hands in her lap. 'Taken a crash course and found out if I'd got the makings of a business woman.'

He didn't quite know what to make of that. Then he decided she'd wanted a new toy to play with and was glad he'd given her the plain facts from the start. If he'd tried to break things gently she might have held back from selling, and that could only have got her deeper into debt.

'It would not have been a good idea,' he said very firmly. He didn't imagine Harriet's talents would be much use in a business world, and he was probably right. If everything had been runing smoothly she might have been able to take over, but she was no industrial whizz-kid.

'Can you sell factories these days?' she asked. 'If business is so bad who'll want it?'

'There have been enquiries.' Mr Snelson cheered up because this was the good news. 'One from a Dutch firm and another from a local man.'

'Who?' Harriet sat up at that.

'Mr Gaul,' said Mr Snelson. 'Jotham Gaul.'

'Oh.' Harriet sat back again, as far as she could go into her chair, and for the first time her frown was really deep. 'Him!'

'You know him, of course?' Mr Snelson was puzzled by the asperity in Harriet's voice, especially when she said,

'Not well, no.' Her face was smooth again, perhaps he had imagined the scowl. Perhaps it only meant that she was thinking.

She was. She knew more about Jotham Gaul than she knew about most of them. His name was the name from around here that cropped up regularly, because he was successful business news. New factories, big orders. In the last five years she had read a fair amount about him and she had met him a few times. Briefly, always by accident, every meeting confirming her first impression of instant abiding dislike.

'Mr Gaul's offer is the better one,' Mr Snelson informed her, and she thought—It would be. She asked,

'How much better?'

'There's the matter of redundancy pay.' This was the bad news again and Mr Snelson's expression was grave. 'You've upward of a hundred employees. Some of them have been there twenty, twenty-five years. They'll be entitled to substantial settlements unless you can offer them alternative employment.'

He paused, as though she might not understand this, and she nodded. 'The Dutch company wants the buildings but not many of the workers,' he explained, 'while Mr Gaul is prepared to take on a much higher proportion of staff.'

Harriet couldn't hold back a sigh. She wished it had been the other way round, and Mr Snelson was looking puzzled again.

'May I ask why you're unwilling to deal with Mr Gaul? He has a very high reputation in industry.'

'I'm sure he has,' said Harriet dryly. 'And if we have to sell obviously we must take the better offer, but I would like to think about it for a while.'

'Of course,' said Mr Snelson, 'and these enquiries reached us before the business was actually put on the market. As soon as the sale becomes official we could receive other offers.'

'I hope so,' said Harriet.

She went out into the garden to do her thinking, and

Mr Snelson went to tell his wife. 'I wish Henry had warned the girl. She wanted to carry on, she didn't want to sell.'

Ida Snelson looked through the French windows at the tall restless figure, with the mane of gleaming hair, pacing backwards and forwards across her lawn. 'A new toy?' she said, and her husband beamed at her.

'Exactly my sentiments,' he said. 'Harriet is even less used to hard work than Henry was.'

But ever since her father had died Harriet had felt that playtime was over, that it was time to start work. It didn't look as though she was going to get the chance here. She stood by the sundial and read the carved inscription round the edge, 'It is later than you think,' and smiled wryly. That was a cheering sentiment. At twenty-two she had hardly missed the boat, even if it was too late to save the family firm.

She went on walking, putting off the time when she would have to go back into the house and agree that Mr Snelson should tell whoever had to be told that the factory was for sale.

'We may receive other offers,' he had said, but if Jotham Gaul wanted it he would probably get it. The way things stood she couldn't afford the pleasure of thwarting him, although there was no man she knew that she would rather say 'No' to.

She had been introduced to him at that New Year's Eve party. Nigel had said, 'Come and meet Jotham Gaul.'

'That's an outlandish name.' She had laughed 'Where on earth does he come from?' and a man had said, 'Yorkshire.'

He towered over Nigel, built like a stevedore, with shoulders that seemed to strain his dinner jacket. A great hulk of a man who might have been none the worse for that if he had been smiling. Every man that night had smiled admiringly at her when they were introduced, but he didn't. He gave her a cool weighing look, and for a moment the shield of her beauty had shattered as though he saw her plain and fat and unloved.

She had wanted to turn away right then, but she had had to stay while Nigel explained that Gaul was a friend of the family and a man to watch. Something about some works up north that were booming, and she had drawled, 'A man to watch? Fascinating!'

'Oh, I am.' His grin was no admiring smile when he added, 'And aren't you the fab girl to watch?'

That was the headline in the magazine, which her father had been showing around that Christmas. It had been flattering, making her feel like a celebrity, but this man wasn't impressed. He thought she was dim, and anyhow she was not the least little bit interested in him. She began to talk about the house.

Nigel had brought her into the dining room, looking for Jotham Gaul. At the far end was a big stone fireplace, carved intricately, and she had babbled, 'Isn't it lovely, this room, this house? I'd love to live in a house like this.'

She had heard Jotham Gaul chuckle. 'Look out, Nigel, I think she's planning to marry you!'

Everyone had laughed. Nigel had said he'd be delighted and Harriet had blushed scarlet, her untried sophistication no match for this kind of teasing.

Jotham Gaul hadn't spoiled the party for her. It had been a night of triumph, but she had disliked him intensely and never wanted to set eyes on him again.

Although Nigel had been right. Of all the guests at that New Year's Eve party at Tudor House Gaul was the high flyer. His rise had been swift and sure and solid. He was in the tycoon bracket now, owning several factories, one about thirty miles away from here.

If he bought her factory she hoped it could all be done through solicitors. She didn't want to meet him unless she had to. They had bumped into each other four times in the last five years and she could recall each occasion very clearly. He seemed to go out of his way to take a rise out of her. God, he was an irritating boor!

She was still walking aimlessly around the garden when Mrs Snelson came to tell her there was a phone call for her, and she went back into the house to speak to Nigel.

When he enquired how she was she said, 'Not so bad, but I've been hearing that the factory is on the rocks.'

He murmured something sympathetic and she asked, 'Did you know?'

'I knew there was talk about your father selling out.'

Local people would know. The men and women who worked there would have heard rumours and known the situation. But her father had never discussed it with her. 'It's thrown me a little,' she admitted. 'I'd started to make plans about staying down here and learning what it was all about.'

'Perhaps you'll still stay down here.'

'Not much point in that now, is there?'

'We could talk about it,' said Nigel. 'Can I come round and fetch you?'

'Yes, please.' Harriet was smiling as she walked away from the phone, and when Nigel had her sitting beside him in his car he looked at her as though the sight of her knocked him out.

'You're the most stunning girl I've ever come across,' he said suddenly. 'And do you know you get more beautiful?'

She was used to compliments, but Nigel meant what he was saying and he was what she needed right now. Somebody nice to talk to, to stop her thinking about her father and this upset about the family business.

She was looking forward to seeing Tudor House again. She had been in fabulous homes all over the world, but if she could have chosen one for her own she would have picked Nigel's home. She couldn't have explained why she coveted that house, but she did, and she leaned forward eagerly in her seat as they drove through the gates and up the drive.

They had been talking about her flat in town, where it was, what it was like. When they went into the grey stone lichen-covered house Nigel said, 'You're lucky having somewhere compact and labour-saving. This place takes a fortune in heating alone.'

It was a warm day and the house was warm. There was no one in the entrance hall nor up on the little gallery, and Harriet stood looking around her, feeling as though the house was a fortress, strong and impregnable. She said, 'I'd change with you. I fell in love with this place when I came here to that New Year's Eve party and I'm still in love with it.'

Nigel smiled. 'Do you remember Jotham suggesting you married me to get it?'

That wouldn't have made her blush now. She would have laughed with the rest of them, and she did laugh.

Her laughter was infectious, she was a girl who laughed a lot, although this week there had been no laughter.

He took her through the door into the parlour, both of them still laughing, and said, 'An old friend. It's like old times.'

Jotham Gaul got up from a chair, and she went on giggling for a few seconds out of sheer nervous surprise. 'I was sorry to hear about your father,' he said. 'I'm glad to see you're bearing up so well.'

The giggles stiffened on her lips and nausea rose in her. Hateful man, she thought, *hateful* ...

CHAPTER TWO

EVERY time she saw Jotham Gaul Harriet's reaction had been to get away from him. In the last five years she had spotted him twice without him seeing her. Once walking along Regent Street, when she had shot into Hamley's before he reached her; and once going into a restaurant in Cheltenham—that time she had ducked down, practically creeping into a seat with her back towards him and a pillar in between them.

She would do a lot to avoid Jotham Gaul because the times they had met, face to face, had been little short of maddening.

Nigel was beaming at them both, asking, 'How long is it since we were all here? Doesn't she look even more beautiful than she did then?'

Jotham grinned and didn't speak, and Harriet said brightly, 'You're putting on weight, aren't you?'

Men with frames like his often ran to fat, but his bulk looked hard and muscular. She wouldn't care to come up against it. 'You're not,' he said. 'You still look hungry.'

'Grey hairs too,' she said.

His hair was short, and unruly as a schoolboy's, and shot with grey. He must have been born with a rough-hewn face. He must have been an ugly baby. He was only a year or two older than Nigel, but the lines from nose to mouth and scoring across the forehead were deep. It was a face with humour and strength, a face that made her hackles rise. She could feel the nerves tightening up the back of her neck as Jotham went on grinning.

'Isn't this nice?' he said.

'Fantastic,' she said. About the only thing in his favour was that you could see him coming. Apart from his height, which got him head and shoulders above most crowds, he was a colourful dresser. He wore a jacket now in a virulent blue tartan and an emerald green polo-necked sweater. Harriet wouldn't have been surprised if he'd been in tartan pants instead of sober grey. Some time she must ask him if he was colour blind. 'What are you doing here?' she asked.

'They let me use a couple of rooms.'

'That's kind,' she said.

'Jotham is family,' said Nigel. 'Always has been.' He went to the sideboard, pouring drinks without asking, handing her a sweet Martini with lemonade. 'I remembered,' he said, and she sipped it and smiled.

She was seventeen when she had dated Nigel. Her tastes had changed, but it was easier to pretend they hadn't because it would have been good to put back the clock. The in-between years hadn't been all that wonderful. She didn't have all that much to show for them.

She asked, 'And you're still farming?' He'd already told her he was, she just liked the sound of it. There was something unchanging about life around here.

'Still a farmer,' said Nigel. He sat down beside her on the sofa and Jotham sat in a big plum-coloured armchair that clashed fiercely with his jacket. Couldn't he see he was in the way?

Well, Harriet wanted him to get up and go; Nigel seemed to think they made a cosy threesome. He said, 'Jotham's the one who's made the money,' sounding only a little envious, and Harriet said coolly, 'We all know he's a captain of industry.'

'And you're a top model,' said Nigel.

'Nowhere near the top.' She didn't admit that often, but

she didn't mind telling Nigel, although it was Jotham who demanded with a leer,

'Why not? With your natural advantages?'

'Because I've got this low boredom threshold,' she snapped.

'I'm sure you have,' he drawled. 'Is that why you haven't married?'

'Could be. Why haven't you?'

She had noticed when she first met him that whoever she was with, whatever was happening, he got to her, blocking out everything else. When she was in that restaurant she hadn't enjoyed a mouthful of her meal because she had been so conscious that he was sitting a few yards away.

... The first time, after the New Year's Eve party, she had just broken off her first engagement and she was at Stratford races with a horsey young man when Jotham Gaul had loomed up in the enclosure.

He had shaken her heartily by the hand and congratulated her, although she would have bet he knew that the engagement had ended and her companion was not her ex-fiancé. That had thrown her, and it hadn't pleased her companion, who was on to a losing streak that day. He was ripping up his tote ticket when Jotham had tapped her shoulder and shaken her hand. Looking at the torn ticket on the ground, Jotham shook his head and remarked, 'With those eyes you've got to be among the winners.'

She said, 'Well, thank you,' because it had sounded like a compliment until he'd added,

'Greedy eyes.'

Then he gave her a tip for the next race, and went off with a very elegant girl who had dived through the crowd towards him. Of course she hadn't bet on the horse, and of course it had won....

'Never in one place long enough,' said Jotham, in answer to why wasn't he married.

'Sad,' she said. 'All this globe-trotting spoiling your love life.'

'Not at all.' He looked at her as though she was missing the point completely. 'Globe-trotting rules out marriage, but it's highly stimulating for your love life. Surely you've found that.'

He might be attractive to some women. Money and power turned most women on, but Jotham Gaul could be rich as Croesus and Harriet would still dodge down side streets to avoid him.

She looked at Nigel and asked, 'Why aren't you married?' She couldn't care less why Jotham was still a bachelor, but she would be interested in Nigel's reasons.

'I've been waiting for you,' he said rather predictably.

He smiled and he wasn't serious, but it would be nice if he still had a hankering for her. Most men had, and she was free as air at the moment. She could think of worse things than getting involved with Nigel, and her lips curved in the mockery and promise she had used with devastating effect ever since she first practised it in a mirror in the ablutions at school.

'By the way,' said Jotham, 'how's the man who makes models out of tins? I saw a photograph of you at the opening of his exhibition.'

Anthony had had an exhibition at the little gallery that Harriet had helped to finance. He was an up-and-coming artist, and he and Harriet had gone around together regularly during the last few months. 'Fine,' she said, 'just fine.'

'You're still very good friends, are you?'

It was common knowledge, there was never any secret about Harriet's affairs, but the affair with Anthony was over now. 'That died the death,' she shrugged, and wished she had put it differently, because what had finished it completely was that he hadn't come to her father's funeral.

She had been making excuses not to see him before then,

getting bored, finding him too possessive, and when the news came through about her father's death Anthony had rushed to her side and been as sympathetic as anybody could be.

He'd offered to come down with her for the funeral, but she'd said no. She'd explained that she would be staying with the Snelsons, and friends who had known her father would be bringing her back; and Anthony had said if she was sure about that he'd be waiting for her in London.

But, unreasonably, she had felt he should have known that she needed all the support she could get, when she stood in that little churchyard saying goodbye to her father for the last time.

'Will you be staying down here?' Jotham was asking her, and Nigel looked anxious, waiting for her reply.

'I might have done if the factory had been paying its way,' she said. 'I had no idea it wasn't. I haven't seen the place for years.'

'You just drew the money?' said Jotham.

'How do you know that?'

He shrugged broad shoulders. 'I've met a few of the men you've been around with.'

She couldn't see the connection, but it had to be insulting and she demanded hotly, 'What does that mean?'

'That you're a grabber who doesn't always give value for money,' he said blandly, and Nigel gasped,

'Hey, now——'

Nigel was going to defend her, but she laughed harshly. 'Look who's talking! I bet you never missed a chance in your life, and until I try to grab from you you can——'

'You try to grab from me and I'll tan the hide off you,' Jotham's deep voice drowned hers. 'Metaphorically speaking, of course.'

'Whatever that means.' Her eyes were brilliant with shining rage. 'My, but you're a big talker.'

'You haven't heard anything yet,' he promised, and Nigel put in,

'What goes on? What started this?'

'I don't know,' said Harriet, 'but I don't like your friend. I never did like him.'

Jotham was laughing and Nigel demanded, 'Is this some sort of joke? You don't even know each other do you? I mean——'

'We've bumped into each other from time to time,' said Jotham. 'Surely I mentioned it.'

'Yes,' said Nigel. 'But——'

'Passed the time of day,' added Jotham. 'Just a few words.'

'That's right,' said Harriet. 'A few words that went a long way.' She was on her feet and so was Jotham, and she couldn't recall when either of them had stood up. 'Goodbye,' she said. 'It's been a tonic meeting you. It always is.'

'You're not going,' said Nigel.

'Is he?'

'I do have some work to do,' said Jotham. He picked up the glass of whisky Nigel had handed him, which was balanced on the wide arm of the armchair. 'You know I made an offer for your factory?'

'Mr Snelson just told me.'

'Well?'

'You mean—am I going to sell to you?' Harriet heard herself squeaking. 'I'd rather burn the place down.'

'No, you wouldn't,' he said cheerfully. 'And you won't get a better offer.' That silenced her long enough for him to get out of the room or she would have thrown something at him. She was left staring at the door, then she rounded on Nigel croaking, 'What do you see in that man? How can you *stand* him? He's an oaf, a great hulking moronic——' she groped for the word and Nigel said plaintively,

'But everybody likes Joth.'

'You're joking!'

He modified that. 'Well, nearly everybody. He can be overpowering, but he's one in a million.'

'Isn't he just?' she drawled, but her heart was thumping and she was shaking and she hadn't felt like this since she was a child, racked by those terrible frustrating rages. She still had a hot temper, but it was years since she had come so close to violence.

She unclenched her clenched hands and said with forced calm, 'Well, I can't stand him. Every time I've met him he's gone out of his way to make me feel an idiot.'

'I'm sorry.' Why, she wondered, was Nigel apologising when he'd done nothing? 'I can't think why,' Nigel went on. 'He can be one of the kindest men you could meet. Mind you, he's nobody's fool and he's never been one for suffering fools.'

Harriet's lips twitched. 'That's it, then.'

'What?' Nigel's embarrassment, as he realised what he had said, widened her smile. His words fell over themselves trying to put things right. 'I didn't mean that you were a fool—lord no, you know I didn't. Nothing like that. I mean that Joth——'

She was laughing now, reassuring him, 'It's all right. He thinks I'm a fool, I think he's a moron. I'll keep out of his way and he'd better keep out of mine.'

With her green eyes, and her red hair and her crackling vitality, it seemed to Nigel that she lit up that dark-panelled room. She was a challenging girl, with her reputation for wildness. His mother hadn't been too happy about him phoning her just now, but when he saw her yesterday the old infatuation had awoken.

When she was seventeen everywhere he had taken her heads had turned, almost every man he knew was envying him. When she went away, to live in London, he wasn't surprised. That was where her father lived most of the time. When his letter went unanswered and he couldn't get her on the telephone he was bitterly hurt but not surprised.

She got engaged, but he had lost her months before that, and although he saw her photographs sometimes, and heard news of her, he hadn't seen her in the flesh for years. When he spoke to her in the churchyard he had been unprepared for the impact the pale pure face, framed by the dark hat, had had on him.

She was lovelier than she had been at seventeen, and he was like a boy with a crush instead of a man of thirty. Life had treated him well enough, and the future promised more of the same—moderate prosperity, good friends. But there hadn't been much excitement.

What there was had mostly come through his friendship with Jotham Gaul, who generated excitement. Nigel looked on Jotham as his best friend. He admired him and envied him. He wouldn't have been human if he hadn't been envious, and now that Harriet was laughing and the atmosphere was easy again Nigel was glad she couldn't stand Jotham. He could do without a rival like that.

He asked, 'What are you going to do about the factory?'

'Sell it,' she said, promptly but with regret. 'What else can I do?'

He had no suggestions. She could have to sell and then she would go away again, and that thought dismayed him. 'Will you go back to London?' he asked.

'I suppose so.'

With most girls he might have suggested she looked for work down here, and offered to ask around and help her. But Harriet was too glamorous for a commonplace job. All he could hope was that she would keep in touch and they could meet sometimes.

He looked at her with eyes that reminded her of a spaniel's and asked, 'Will you be coming here again?'

'It won't be that easy.' She grimaced, wrinkling the perfect nose. 'I don't have a car. I lost my licence a couple of months ago—speeding.'

'Can I see you if I come up to London?' He sat down on the sofa, drawing her down beside him, and the spaniel eyes were brown and gentle. 'Now that we have met again,' he begged, 'please don't slip out of my life a second time.'

She would have promised that, and she would have kissed him because he deserved kissing, looking as though her promise mattered so desperately. But as she leaned towards him the door opened and his mother came into the room.

Nigel's mother was thin and colourless. Harriet remembered her always dressed in beige and pale muddy shades, with light brown hair and a worried face. Sylvia Joliffe's main worry in those days had been that Nigel was fascinated by Harriet Brookes who, in his mother's opinion, was much more likely to break a man's heart than make him a good wife.

When Harriet went away Sylvia Joliffe had breathed a silent prayer of thanks, and another prayer that Harriet wouldn't come back again.

Of course she had been shocked to hear of Henry Brooke's death, and she was sorry for his daughter. She had gone along to the funeral, but that evening she had overheard Nigel phoning to cancel his evening date. He had talked about Harriet for hours, wondering what her plans were, and Sylvia Joliffe had started looking worried again.

Harriet was presumably here for the rest of the day. Nigel had phoned her and then told his mother that he was fetching her, and Sylvia Joliffe came into the room wearing her hostess smile, with a nervous tic twitching the side of her mouth.

It hadn't helped seeing Nigel and Harriet holding hands and Harriet's lips about an inch from his cheek.

'Hello, Harriet,' said Sylvia Joliffe. 'How lovely to see you again,' and her heart sank like a stone. She had seen the magazines and the commercials, and she had seen Harriet pale in her black yesterday. But now there was a faint rose glow on the girl's high cheekbones and the full proud mouth looked a soft temptation for any man.

The green eyes were enough to hypnotise, and Sylvia Joliffe thought that her son stood about as much chance as a rabbit before a dancing python. She said, 'We were very sorry about your father.'

So was I, thought Harriet. He had a hundred faults, but I loved him. More than he loved me. She said, 'Thank you,' and she was glad that Nigel still held her hand. She was feeling lonely of late.

'Will you be staying down here long?' Sylvia Joliffe knew about the factory, there would be that business to settle and Nigel had told her Harriet was staying with the Snelsons. But she longed to hear that the stay would be brief. There wasn't much for a girl like Harriet Brookes around here. Except Nigel, perhaps. Oh, please not Nigel, his mother prayed.

'A few days,' said Harriet, and Nigel offered eagerly,

'Why don't you come to us? It can't be much fun for you at the Snelsons! Not that it's fun you're looking for at a time like this, of course, but you like this house, don't you, and there's plenty of room. Isn't there plenty of room?' He turned to his mother, who began to stammer objections.

Harriet couldn't just walk out on the Snelsons. Tudor House was not nearly as comfortable as the Snelson's modern home. The rooms that weren't used hadn't been used in ages. Of course Harriet was welcome, they'd love to have her staying here, but ... but ...

Harriet hardly heard her. She rarely listened to things she didn't want to hear, and she had known there was no welcome from Nigel's mother when she had seen the twitch in her cheek.

But she had been invited to move into Tudor House for a few days and she said, 'Oh yes, please,' and Nigel beamed although it had very little to do with him. It was the house. She wanted to stay here while she sorted herself out.

There were decisions to be made about the factory, and about herself, and this house was wonderfully peaceful and she had this feeling of affinity with it.

She said fervently, 'I would love to stay with you,' and saw Nigel actually start to blush under the tan of his skin. 'Thank you,' she said to his mother, and Mrs Joliffe's compressed lips tightened even more.

'When would you like to come?' Sylvia Joliffe asked coldly, and Nigel said, 'Right now, I'll take her back to fetch her things.'

'I don't know what the Snelsons are going to think.' Sylvia Joliffe was pleading a lost cause. 'I only hope they won't be offended.'

'I'm sure they won't,' said Harriet, and Nigel stood up as she did.

'Then I suppose I'd better see about a bedroom for you,' said his mother, looking martyred. She had never liked Harriet Brookes, and this certainly showed that Harriet had no regard at all for anyone else's feelings. She was the last girl his mother wanted for Nigel. 'Don't forget to phone Annie,' said Sylvia Joliffe to her son. 'Didn't you tell her last night that you'd phone her today?'

Nigel glared furiously. While he had been talking on the phone in the hall his mother must have been eavesdropping, although all he could do about that now was to say, 'There's no rush,' and guide Harriet out of the room.

Harriet was rather amused. Nigel's girl-friends wouldn't worry her, there weren't many girls she couldn't outshine, but when they got into the car she asked, 'Who's Annie?'

because she knew he expected her to.

'A girl,' he said, turning on the ignition and crashing the gears.

'Aren't we all?' said Harriet. 'Is she important?'

'My mother would like her to be.' Nigel didn't say that until yesterday he had been content to drift towards the time when he would ask Annie to marry him. Seeing Harriet again had put Annie out of mind. He wouldn't be phoning her today because he had nothing to say to her. Harriet filled his thoughts.

Mrs Snelson said goodbye to her guest and remembered that Nigel had been very gone on Harriet when she'd lived here years ago. Now she had been invited to stay at Tudor House, and Mrs Snelson felt sorry for Annie Hughes, who couldn't hold a candle to Harriet for looks but was a very nice girl.

'Do you think we could drive to the factory?' asked Harriet as the car drew away from the Snelsons' home.

'You're the boss,' said Nigel, and she smiled wryly.

'Not for long.'

'I wasn't talking about the factory.' Nigel looked at her at every opportunity, stealing a quick sidewards glance now as they coasted along the straight almost empty road. 'I meant anything you want, just give the orders.'

She laughed, tossing back her head, and he breathed the scent from her hair and his breath caught as though she had put her lips against his. Harriet knew exactly the effect she was having. A lot of it was deliberate, the toss of her hair, the smile, the sweep of dark lashes looking up at him. Tricks.

'You're perfect,' said Nigel. 'My God, but you're beautiful!'

She wasn't perfect, but she was beautiful, and that was why Nigel, and the others, wanted to give her anything she wanted. Jotham had said she was a grabber, but he didn't know what he was talking about, and anyway, why was she thinking about him? She said, 'It must be about ten years since I was there last, and now it's going to be sold, I'm on my way to see it. Crazy!'

The factory was on the outskirts of a small town a few miles away, and she looked for familiar landscapes as they drove along. There were plenty of changes, and for some reason that depressed her, although she had expected them. They passed the hotel where her father had always stayed and she said, 'They made him very comfortable there. He liked living in hotels.'

'Do you?' Nigel asked.

'Not much. This last day or two I've started wishing I had a real home. I think I might get out of the flat, find somewhere.'

'What are you looking for?' They were held up by traffic lights, and she turned away, scanning the shops and the passers-by.

'I don't know,' she said at last. 'If I find it maybe I'll know.'

When they reached the factory it was closing time. Workers were streaming through the gates and a single line of cars edged out into the road slowing down the passing traffic. Before Nigel's car reached the gates Harriet had decided against turning in. If she went in what could she do? Talk to men she didn't know about selling out? Some of the staff had spoken to her in the churchyard, but not about their jobs, although that problem must have been uppermost in their minds.

She said, 'There's really no point in me going in, is there? I'll phone Mr Snelson tomorrow.'

'You'll take Joth's offer?'

'If we can't get a better one.'

'You won't, you know.' Nigel sounded so positive that she asked him,

'How do you know?'

'Because he always gets what he wants,' said Nigel.

They went slowly past the gates and from here everything looked exactly the same. 'And he called me a grabber,' she muttered. 'I wish I could afford to tell him what to do with his offer! Do me a favour, don't mention him again. That was my father's office, the window above the main doorway.' She didn't know why she told Nigel that, it was of no interest to him, but as her eyes fixed on the window she remembered the room, the thick moss-green carpet, the leather armchair behind the polished desk, and on the desk the photograph of her mother in a silver frame.

The last time she was in there was the summer after her mother died. She was home on holiday from school, and she had hardly seen her father. She had gone over to the factory because he had said he would take her out to lunch, but when she arrived something had turned up and instead she had lunched with his secretary.

She sighed and Nigel said gently, 'I know how you feel. You were very close, weren't you?' That was what they all thought, but if her father had loved her he would have found time to spend that lunch hour with her.

'Where shall we go now?' Nigel mused, and she said, 'Surprise me.'

He wished he could, whisking her off somewhere that would outdo anywhere she had ever been, and astonishing her with his wit and charm. There wasn't much hope of that, but they drove around for a while, and he enjoyed having her with him. Her scent and the feel of her close to him made his blood race. She was a gorgeously sexy girl, and he could think of nothing he wanted more in the world than the chance to make love to her.

He took her for a meal to a three-star spot he knew well and that was well known. Upstairs was a carvery. Downstairs were the cellars where a disco played.

He had been heading for the carvery which led direct from the foyer, with crystal chandeliers and an atmosphere of leisured affluence. But Harriet held back, listening, then asked, 'Where's the music coming from? Is there dancing?'

'Would you like that?'

Nigel would have preferred to sit at one of those quiet tables and talk to her and look at her, but she was on her way down the stairs, taking it for granted that he would follow. At least they managed to get a table against the wall, far enough away from the beat of the music and the whirling coloured lights to be able to concentrate on each other. The food down here was 'bar snacks', but Harriet wasn't hungry. She toyed with a salad while they ate, 'catching up on the years', she said. Nigel didn't have much to tell, but she did, and he listened as she spun her stories. It all sounded gay and glamorous and he commented, 'You've had a marvellous life, haven't you?'

She laughed. 'It hasn't been bad so far, and I always expect the best is to come. Don't you?'

'I hope so.' Nigel glared at a man who was smiling at her. 'Would you like to dance?'

He was quite a good dancer, he and Annie had been down here only last week, but he hadn't danced with a girl like Harriet before. Annie stayed with her partner and gave the others room, but Harriet took over as though she was the only dancer on the floor, hair and body swaying and sensuous, moving to the beat of the music, becoming part of it.

She didn't need a partner, although every man she passed took a few steps with her. Nigel knew she could have stepped on to that floor alone. She didn't need anybody, just the music. Even in her plain dark dress her body was like a bright fierce flame, always out of his grasp.

She was half recognised more than once. They didn't know her but they had seen her, and mingling with the blare of the music he heard, 'Who is that? ... Do you know who that is? ... Is she an actress?'

He stood on the edge of the dance floor and waited until she had danced her fill, then he took her back to their table. 'Do you dance much?' he asked.

She took a long drink of the white wine that half filled her glass, draining it. 'I enjoyed that,' she said. 'I dance more since I lost my licence.'

'What licence?' Ever since they'd walked from the door to the table Harriet had been getting more than her share of attention. She had walked in as though she owned the place, and she was the most striking girl in the room, so of course people were looking at her. But since she had danced it seemed to Nigel that all eyes were on them and he couldn't make up his mind whether he was embarrassed or flattered.

'My driving licence,' she said. 'When things got on top of me I used to get into my car and put my foot down. Dancing helps. It's another sort of release.'

Her hair was tumbling over her shoulders, she was breathing fast and she was looking wonderful. Nigel wished he had the courage to lean over the table and kiss her parted lips. 'It's been a bad time,' she said.

He patted her hand instead and said, 'I know, I know.' She hoped he wouldn't go on again about how close she and her father had been. Passing the factory had tensed her up, and Nigel had been a super relaxing companion, but he didn't know. Nobody knew.

A man came up to the table and asked, 'Don't I know you?'

'No,' she said.

'I'm sure I've seen you somewhere before.' He was young and handsome and cheerful. He stood his ground, his darting eyes hovering on the soft curve of her breasts.

'You may have seen me,' she said, 'but you don't know

me.' She turned a cold shoulder on him and began to talk to Nigel, and Nigel glared until he went.

Nigel had done more scowling since they came in here tonight than he had ever done escorting Annie. Annie was a pretty girl, but he had never had to hold back her admirers. He asked, 'Does this sort of thing happen often?'

'Sorry.' Harriet rested her chin on latticed fingers, and he saw the smoky smudges over the delicate cheekbones. It was partly her own fault, her dancing had been spectacular. But even if she had sat at this table all evening she would still have had the men staring at her. She had those kind of looks, and she had done just enough modelling for most of them to feel they ought to be recognising her.

'You need someone to look after you,' said Nigel. 'Is there anyone? What about that artist Joth was talking about?'

She shook her head and he could hardly believe his luck. This time he did lean across to kiss her and she reached over too, her lips meeting his half way.

It was late when they got back to Tudor House, although lights were still burning in some of the windows. They garaged the car and walked across to the main doorway carrying her two suitcases. An owl hooted, and something screamed or cried, and Harriet was glad when the heavy door opened and closed after them because it was safe inside.

She was glad she was spending the night here. She would like to wander around the house in the early hours. All alone. Without anyone, even Nigel.

She asked, 'Do you believe in reincarnation?' and while Nigel was puzzling over that, 'Maybe I lived here once. It's my dream house.' She moved around the hall with a fluid dancing grace, and there was no tension in her now. 'Honestly,' she said, 'I have had dreams about it.'

Nigel watched her, smiling. When she had finished floating around he knew that she would come into his arms, and then he caught sight of a white envelope propped up against the phone. He could read his mother's printed writing, large enough to be seen from a distance, 'ANNIE RANG'.

He didn't touch it, but Harriet saw him look towards it. She had tripped up half a dozen stairs and now she was walking slowly down again trailing a hand behind along the balustrade. She said, 'Message from Annie?'

'Yes.'

'Is it too late to phone her?'

'Much too late,' he said, although he had often phoned Annie later than this. She had an extension by her bed and they had had sleepy chats with him in an armchair by the fire in the drawing room. It wasn't the time on the clock that was stopping him. He meant that it had been too late to phone Annie ever since Harriet had come back.

Harriet came down the stairs and across to him. She slipped her hands behind his head and he felt them fastening, holding. She was a tall girl, she only had to tilt her head a little to look into his eyes. 'Thank you,' she said. 'Old friends, and old houses. You know this is like coming home.'

He was starting to say something about hoping she would never go away again when the drawing room door opened silently—it must have been on the jar—and his mother came into the hall.

'Your room's ready, Harriet,' she said, and Harriet kissed Nigel swiftly and softly before she let him go. 'This way,' said Sylvia Joliffe.

'This isn't hotel service,' Nigel protested. 'Which room have you put her in?' but Harriet said,

'I would like to go up, please. It has been a long day.' That was true, she was more than ready to be shown to her room, and she picked up one of her suitcases. Nigel took the other and Sylvia Joliffe went upstairs ahead of them.

She didn't ask where they had been. She didn't say anything at all. They went along corridors and up staircases, silently except for the sound of their footsteps and all the rustles and creaks of the old house, and at last they stopped and Sylvia Joliffe opened a door.

'Why this room?' Nigel demanded.

'The bed was aired,' said his mother coldly, 'and it's a nice room.' She went in and switched on a bedside lamp and stood waiting while Nigel put down the case he was carrying. She wasn't leaving him here, and Harriet said,

'Goodnight, then,' to both of them.

She was used to women guarding their menfolk from her, but she wished that Sylvia Joliffe had been less suspicious. She would have liked to be friends with Nigel's mother.

The room *was* nice, with black beams set in the white walls, and dark solid oak furniture. It was a warm night and the fourposter looked inviting in the lamplight. She hadn't been fooling, this really had been her dream house ever since that New Year's Eve party.

When she thought of the party she thought of her father again and tears filled her eyes. She hardly ever cried—tears made you ugly—but now she allowed herself a little weep before she took off her coat and hung it in the wardrobe.

She was kneeling down, opening a case, when the tap came on the door and she grimaced as she got up. She was tired. She wanted no company but her own until break-fast time, but this had to be Nigel and she must be tactful. Another goodnight kiss, a plea of weariness, and a promise in her smile should send him happily to his own bed.

She turned the knob and opened the door, and the smile that was curving her lips vanished in a flash as Jotham Gaul stepped into the room.

CHAPTER THREE

JOTHAM was the last man she'd expected to find outside her bedroom door at well past midnight. He walked past her and the floorboards creaked, while she practically hung on to the doorknob for support.

'Nigel's mother is worried about you,' he said.

Harriet knew that. She stayed where she was in the doorway demanding, 'And what has it got to do with you?'

They must have been talking about her. After she'd left Nigel's mother must have gone looking for Jotham, although what did she imagine he could do that would have the faintest influence on Harriet?

'Like Nigel said,' added Jotham, 'I've been one of the family for years.'

'Big Brother?' drawled Harriet. 'Isn't he old enough to have a mind of his own?'

'Not while you're around, it seems,' said Jotham.

'So he likes me. Why not? What's wrong with me?' She shouldn't have asked that from a man who was looking at her the way this man was.

'Not much, to the naked eye,' he said cheerfully. 'But I wouldn't touch you with a barge pole. Except in self-defence.'

'You'd better not!' She moved away, leaving the door wide, skirting the room to avoid coming near him, stopping at the dressing table. In the mirror her dark red hair glowed, and she leaned forward to rub a streak of mascara from her cheek. She would have died sooner than let him see she had been crying.

He watched her. 'A face and figure like yours is money

47

in the bank, isn't it?' he said. 'What will you use when your assets run out?'

She felt as though she had been kicked in the stomach, but she managed to say, 'Get out!'

'You'll marry one of them before then, I suppose. Just don't get any ideas about it being Nigel.'

She went on dabbing her face until he closed the door after him and then she turned quickly from the mirror, hating him, with a raw tearing hatred that had her gasping, for telling her that her looks were all she had.

He was right there, she'd always known it, but he was wrong saying she'd lose her looks because she would always be beautiful. Her fingertips ran over jawbone and cheekbones and smooth taut skin, and then she pressed them to her lips to stop the trembling.

She would always be beautiful, but she wouldn't be young for ever, and she was in no state tonight to be forced to face that fact.

How would she survive when she couldn't turn heads any more? There wasn't even money. The factory wouldn't keep her, and she could only model so long as her face was flawless.

Who could she turn to? She had friends and men who said they loved her, but her attraction for them had to be her looks, and her vitality, because she hadn't had many friends when she had been dull and plain. She hadn't had any friends then. Her father might still have cared about her as he grew older too, but she didn't have her father any more. She didn't really have anybody.

She wished it had been Nigel knocking on her door. She wished she knew where Nigel was because, after what Jotham Gaul had just said, she desperately needed reassurance.

She opened the door into the corridor and the next door

was open and Jotham was standing in it. 'Looking for some-body?' he asked.

'Looking for the bathroom.'

'End of the corridor.'

She went swishing past him and she was in the bath-room before she realised that she ought to have been carry-ing a sponge bag to make that excuse credible. No wonder Nigel had been surprised at the room his mother had chosen for Harriet, next door to Jotham's.

She'd said it was because the bed was aired, but the real reason was so that Jotham could keep an eye on Harriet, and Harriet sat on the side of the bath and rubbed her mouth again, with the back of her hand. It was amusing really. He was on guard to keep her and Nigel apart. What was he supposed to do if he heard suspicious sounds next door? Come barging in or bang on the wall? She made her-self smile at that, and after a few moments she was really smiling, and then she began to look around her.

This bathroom was antiquated. It must date from at least the beginning of the century. Everything seemed to be in a dark brown panelled box: the washbasin, the high-sited loo tank, the bath. But the water in the old-fashioned brass taps ran hot, and there was a row of bath salts and lotions on a shelf, and while she was in here she might as well use the amenities.

She bathed and soaked for a while, then wrapped herself in a large soft white towel, carrying her clothes and shoes. She had intended to go quietly to her room, but when she passed the door next to hers she couldn't resist whacking it with the heel of her shoe, and in about half a minute Jotham Gaul stuck out his head and blinked at her.

There was no light on in his room and she hoped she'd woken him up. She said brightly, 'I thought I'd better let you know I'm through with my bath and I'm getting to bed.

You can go to sleep now, unless you're on guard for the night.'

'I've said my piece. That's all I was asked to do.' He blinked again, he had curly lashes enviably thick, then he yawned and Harriet clenched her jaw to stop herself yawning too. 'I shouldn't let him see you with your hair like that,' he said. 'Rat's tails.'

Her hair was damp but it would soon spring into its deep waves, and there was nothing wrong with it now. 'Of course your grey hair doesn't matter,' she retorted. 'Nor that you've got a face only a mother could love. Your charm is money.'

He grinned, 'Money lasts. I intend to be a very rich and sexy octogenarian. Sleep well.'

He shut his door and she went into her room, dropping her armful of clothes on a chair. She closed her door, still clutching the towel around her, then dropped the towel and looked closely at herself in the mirror, as though her slim young body might be thickening.

Her reflection reassured her. There wasn't much wrong yet, except for the frown, and she smoothed that away before she slipped between the sheets in the big soft bed.

She didn't sleep too well. She couldn't remember if she had done any dreaming, but she woke with her hands clenched, curled up, lying on her side and taking hardly more room than a child would have done.

Nigel's mother was bending over her saying, 'A cup of tea, Harriet?'

'Thank you. You shouldn't have bothered. What time is it?' She struggled upright, taking the proffered cup and saucer, pulling the top of the sheet up with her other hand.

'Breakfast's ready when you are,' said Sylvia Joliffe, as though Harriet hadn't spoken, with a disapproving look at the bare shoulders, and Harriet resisted the temptation to ask, 'What does Annie sleep in? Flannelette?'

The cup of tea was almost cold, it must have been poured
out ages ago, and it was plain that Harriet had already over-
stayed her welcome. She didn't hurry downstairs. She
didn't want any breakfast and she liked being in this room.
She dressed slowly. Not that it took long to decide what she
was going to wear. She hadn't brought much in the way of
clothes, and everything she had brought was plain and no
bright colours.

She put on a grey skirt and a matching sweater, and gun-
metal court shoes, but to Nigel's mother she still looked
like something out of a magazine when she walked into the
kitchen.

It was the flame of her hair, the arrogance in her walk,
as well as her stunning looks, and Sylvia Joliffe looked up
with a distrust she made no effort to hide. Yet if she had
smiled Harriet would have smiled back, and the girl's smile
would have been genuine and friendly.

Sylvia Joliffe was alone at the kitchen table, with a pot
of tea and the newspapers in front of her. This half hour
before her 'daily' arrived was one of her quiet times and
usually she relished it. Usually she drank several cups of
tea and read the newspapers right through to the sports
pages. But the sight of Harriet Brookes set her teeth on
edge, because Harriet could upset today and every day.

She had upset Sylvia already. Nigel had been waiting
for Harriet to come downstairs ever since his mother had
taken up that cup of cold tea. She wouldn't have taken anything up if Nigel hadn't asked her to. He had no idea the
tea was cold, of course, and Sylvia was ashamed of her own
bad manners, but Nigel fretting, and looking at his watch
as though he hated to leave the house without saying good
morning to Harriet had irritated his mother.

When he couldn't hang around any longer he'd said,
'Tell Harriet I'll see her for lunch.'

Sylvia Joliffe got up now and said, 'This is spoiled with standing so long, I'd better cook you some more.' Two rashers, on a plate on the cooker, had congealed and looked tough and unappetising, and Harriet said,

'I'm sorry, but please don't bother, I don't usually eat breakfast.' She hadn't been hungry for days. She had picked at food if it was put in front of her, and if she was left to her own devices she had missed more meals than she had eaten. She had no appetite this morning and Syliva Joliffe clucked disapprovingly, scooping the wasted food into the bin.

'Tea?' she said.

'Thank you.' Harriet poured her own, and the two women sat at the table together, making stilted conversation around the weather and the newspaper headlines. There was no warmth at all. It all sounded like something out of a bad play, and the silences grew longer. After one that dragged on Sylvia asked, 'What are your plans for today?'

Harriet had been looking out of the window at a small white cloud floating by and thinking that she should be phoning Mr Snelson. If Nigel had been here she would have been tempted to ask if she might spend the day on the farm with him, because she would have liked a few carefree hours in the sunshine before getting down to the dreary business of economics.

'Where's Nigel?' she enquired, and Sylvia Joliffe's mouth snapped shut.

'I don't know,' she muttered. 'He was going somewhere to see about some machinery, an auction I think it was, or it could have been a private sale.' She wasn't telling Harriet where Nigel had gone, and she wasn't saying that he'd be back for lunch either. She didn't want Harriet staying here all day. Harriet surely had business to attend to at the factory. Sylvia said, 'Jotham wanted to see you before you left.'

'Again?' said Harriet. 'He was waiting for me last night. You did know that, I suppose?'

A pink blush rose in the older woman's cheeks although she affected nonchalance. 'Was he?'

'Oh, come on,' Harriet had had enough of this. 'Of course you knew. He told me to keep away from Nigel, didn't he? You knew he was going to do that.'

The blush deepened and Sylvia Joliffe fingered her tea-cup, lifting it a couple of inches and then replacing it. 'I didn't expect him to be quite so blunt.'

'Didn't you?' Harriet's voice was sharp because Jotham hadn't stopped at being blunt, he had been brutal. 'What did you expect him to say? As you know him so well I should have thought you'd have known he doesn't waste time being tactful. That was the message, wasn't it? "We don't want you here. Clear off."'

Of course it was, but hearing it threw Sylvia into confusion. She stammered, 'I didn't expect him to—well yes, I talked to him, I always talk things over with Joth, and I was worried.' She drew a hiccupping breath. 'Yes, I was. Nigel couldn't give you the kind of life you're used to. Look at you!' and she sounded as though Harriet was some exotic being from another planet. 'You'd never make a farmer's wife.'

'For pity's sake,' Harriet protested, 'I've only just met him. You can forget the few times we went out together when I was seventeen, because that was a very long time ago. You can say we've only just met and maybe we're going to be friends, but it would take a long time again before the question of marriage came up. If it ever did.'

Nigel's mother wasn't reassured. She sat there, practically wringing her hands, and wailing, 'He's got such a nice girl. It would be terrible if he let her down, and she'd make him such a good wife.'

'And I wouldn't?' Harriet said drily.

'You know you wouldn't. You're a——' Harriet waited, dark eyebrows arched to hear what she was, and Sylvia Joliffe said, 'You're a girl who could marry a millionaire. Somebody like Joth you could marry.'

Harriet started to laugh, 'That would be a fate worse than death!' and Sylvia Joliffe burst into tears as Jotham Gaul walked into the kitchen.

He went to Sylvia, putting a hand on her shoulder and patting it, and glared at Harriet. 'You've got a great sense of humour, haven't you?'

'It's a very funny life,' said Harriet. What else could she do, to a suggestion that she might marry somebody like Joth, except laugh? Sylvia Joliffe was upset, but she was managing to be very offensive.

'I'm glad you think so,' he said. This morning he was wearing a lumberjack shirt in a black and red check, black pants and a black cord jacket, and he looked bigger than ever, bending over Sylvia, who was sniffing now and smiling weakly. 'I'm sorry,' she said, wiping her eyes, 'I was being silly.'

'You were,' Harriet agreed, and got another glare from Joth, who had eyes like flint when he looked at her, but whose expression changed completely when he smiled down at Sylvia. 'It's all right,' he said, and Harriet sat back, smouldering with anger.

By 'All right' he meant—don't bother about Harriet Brookes. I'll see she causes no trouble.

And Nigel's mother—who had taken no notice when Harriet tried to reassure her—brightened, and smiled back at Joth as though he was her second son. 'I'm a silly old woman,' she said. 'I must clear the table. Maisie's due any minute.' She got up in a flurry of activity, and caught the milk jug with her elbow, sending it spinning and the milk spilling all over the *Daily Mail*. 'Oh dear!' she ran for a mopping cloth. 'I can see it's going to be one of those days.'

'It surely got off to a good start,' agreed Harriet, and Jotham asked,

'Can I give you a lift anywhere?'

'I haven't made up my mind where I'm going.' Wherever it was she would need transport. Unless she postponed all decisions until later and walked around the farm and through the lanes this morning. She looked out of the window again, at the blue sky, and Joth said,

'Well, you can't stay here. Sylvia doesn't share your sense of humour.'

Harriet had never been asked to leave a house before, and she was not Jotham Gaul's guest but Nigel's and she could have been highly indignant. But she was not on form these days and suddenly she was tired. She didn't want to fight anybody. She got up, pushing back her chair, and said quietly, 'Give me five minutes to pack and then perhaps you'll take me to a station where I can get a train to London.'

'Oh no,' Sylvia Joliffe almost dropped the tray she was carrying, 'you can't do that! I didn't mean that. What should I say to Nigel?'

'You might tell him you asked me to leave and Jotham kindly ran me to the station,' said Harriet, and couldn't resist adding, 'Tell him to ring me some time.'

Nigel would probably follow her, and serve them both right. 'Jotham!' Sylvia Joliffe wailed, and a woman passed the kitchen window and nodded and smiled. 'Maisie!' Sylvia screeched on an even more desperate note. Sylvia Joliffe's 'daily' loved a good gossip. If she got any idea of the situation here it would be common knowledge tomorrow.

'Come on, Beauty,' said Jotham. 'Let's talk while you pack.'

He went ahead. He would be waiting for her, Harriet supposed, outside their bedroom doors. If she was Beauty she wouldn't have to look far for the Beast. Oh, why did he have to be here? Why couldn't Nigel's mother have been friendlier? All Harriet had wanted was to stay a little while in this house, with folk who might have been old friends.

She walked slowly, but at last she had to arrive at the corridor where Jotham was waiting. It wasn't all that wide. It wouldn't be easy to pass him without brushing against him, and when she reached him he put an arm across, blocking her way. 'Before you start packing,' he said, 'this is not a joke. Sylvia in tears is not funny.'

When he'd walked into the kitchen it must have looked as though she was laughing at the weeping woman, and she almost flinched from the grimness in his face. 'I wasn't laughing because she was crying,' she protested, 'I was laughing at something she said.'

'She didn't think it was amusing.'

'I don't think she meant it to be, but it was the funniest thing I've heard in years.'

She thought for a moment that he was going to hit her. He took a half step towards her and she backed to the wall and he stood with flat palms against the panelling, arms full length and Harriet pinned between them. 'Well,' she said shrilly, 'does she want me out of this house or doesn't she?'

'She wants you out of Nigel's life.'

This was one of the few men with whom she needed to throw her head right back if she was going to look up at him this close. If she didn't she was staring at the top undone button of his shirt. 'That much I've gathered,' she said.

'He fell for you pretty badly last time. You never answered a letter, you wouldn't take a phone call. He went to pieces over you.' He was accusing her, she was being blamed, but she knew that nothing like that had ever happened to him over a woman, and she stopped herself just in time from saying, 'It takes all sorts.' He made her so nervous that she could only think flippantly, but she would be a fool to provoke him and she said, 'Well, I'm sorry, but that was a long time ago.'

'Your record doesn't suggest that you've changed much.' She clasped her hands behind her and held them tight, with her shoulders back. That was the only way she could avoid touching or being touched. She stood ramrod straight between his arms. 'This is my family,' Jotham said. 'I don't want them hurt.'

'I don't want to hurt anybody.' All she had wanted was to stay a little while because she would have liked a home like this house. 'And you're lucky you've got a family,' she added, 'even if you did have to adopt them.'

She had nobody now, and some of the hardness went out of his face, and his arms dropped. 'I don't like to see Sylvia upset,' he said, 'and I think you would be very bad news for Nigel, but I apologise if I seem to be using bullying tactics.'

At a time like this, he meant, just after she had lost her father. He meant everything he'd said, but perhaps he should have put it more gently. She didn't move for a moment. She stayed tense, hands clasped behind her, head thrown back, pressed against the wall; and it was like it was the first time he'd looked at her at the New Year's Eve party. Then he saw the plain girl under the beautiful skin. Now it seemed that he knew her father had only valued her after she grew into a beauty. When she was a lonely and frightened child nobody would have landed her father with Harriet.

What it really meant was that Jotham Gaul had a way of looking at her as though she was a phoney, and she glared back at him. 'Not that I should think you'd intimidate easily,' he said. He didn't smile, he wasn't complimenting her.

'If you put your mind to it,' she said coldly, 'you could probably intimidate King Kong. May I go now?' He stepped back from her door. 'I would like to stay today,' she said. 'I do have to see Mr Snelson.'

She didn't anticipate any objection. Nigel's mother had panicked at the prospect of telling Nigel that Harriet had gone without even saying goodbye. Tomorrow would probably suit her better, and Harriet felt that after seeing Mr Snelson and dealing with that dreary business she would like to spend a last evening with Nigel. He deserved some consideration, especially as that would be the end of their reunion.

'All right,' said Joth. 'I'll take you.'

She said, 'I could get a taxi. Don't you have to go to work?'

'This is work. I want your factory.' Nobody could accuse him of being a hypocrite. Or missing a trick. She said, 'I would like very much to say you can't have it.'

In the bedroom she picked out a light cashmere coat and looked at her reflection in the wardrobe mirror, because that was what she usually did when she was feeling depressed. It usually cheered her, although the day would come when it wouldn't, when wrinkles would mar the smooth skin. She could see where they would be. They were there already, very faintly, and she seized her hairbrush and brushed her hair until the electricity crackled. That made her feel better. She tossed her hair back and put on her coat and took another look at herself.

Nigel's mother had been telling her she looked too expensive to be a village farmer's wife. Perhaps she did.

The two men she had been engaged to had both been
wealthy, the first the only son of a man who owned a string
of luxury hotels. That had happened not long after she first
went to London, and he was handsome and weak and very
soon she had handed his ring back. The second had been
about eighteen months ago and lasted, on and off, for six
months.

Perhaps she wasn't the marrying kind. Both Jotham Gaul
and Nigel's mother seemed very sure she would make Nigel
unhappy. They both remembered the last time, when she
had left here and Nigel. He had sent her letters, and rung
her day and night at first. But he had been followed by a
number of men who thought that Harriet was the loveliest
girl they knew, and in the whirl of life she had almost forgotten him.

She was sure, too, that he had almost forgotten her until
they met again a couple of days ago. Now he was falling for
her once more and she would have encouraged that because
it would have been comforting and pleasant, but she didn't
want to give his mother a nervous breakdown, and she
didn't want Jotham Gaul deciding he had a grievance
against her. That pay-off would be tougher than she could
handle.

There was no sign of Jotham when she came out of her
room, a few minutes later, and no sign of Sylvia when she
reached the ground floor, using the main staircase and coming into the hall. It was a lovely house. Why couldn't they
let her stay a little while? If I do ever marry a millionaire,
she thought, I'll ask him to buy this house for us to live in,
and she laughed at herself because that was an impossible
dream.

The front door was slightly ajar, sunshine streamed in,
so bright after the shadows in the house that she was
dazzled when she stepped outside. She raised a hand to

shade her eyes and saw the car, drawn up, with Jotham at the wheel.

It was a gleaming Porsche in mocha black. 'Nice,' she commented, as she slipped into the passenger seat. She touched the tan leather upholstery with her long pearl-tipped fingers and Jotham said,

'Don't tell me, but I'm sure you could find someone to buy you one.'

'Funny you should say that. I was just wondering if I could find somebody to buy me this house.'

'I don't think it's for sale.' He sounded as though she meant that about buying the house, although he knew she wasn't serious, and she said,

'So my only way of getting it would be by marrying Nigel.'

'Do yourself a favour. You could make a fool of Nigel, but not that big a fool. He isn't going to marry you.'

Of course he wasn't. If he asked her she would say no. She had never even considered marrying Nigel, but she wasn't setting Jotham Gaul's mind at rest easily. She smiled an enigmatic smile and he chuckled, 'You over-price yourself, Beauty.'

'How would you know?' she asked, and as he went to turn on the ignition, 'I suppose you wouldn't let me drive?'

She bit her lip hard after that because it was stupid to ask when you knew you were going to be turned down, but she had suddenly yearned to be behind the wheel. 'Are you a good driver?' Jotham asked.

'Very good.' She was skilful and experienced and she had always loved cars. Her trouble was she had driven too fast, but she would go very carefully indeed if he let her take the wheel now.

'Let's see how you start her off,' he said, and he got out of the car and adjusted the seat and Harriet moved across. She hadn't expected this for a second. He probably thought that she would crash gears and he could wince and say, 'You're not much use, are you? Purely ornamental.'

She waited until he was settled in the passenger seat and then she moved off competently, negotiating the drive without a jerk, slowing at the entrance long enough to check the road, and turning right, everything going smooth as silk.

It was a superb machine, handling it gave her an almost sensuous delight. She would have loved to press down on the accelerator and open up. It was frustrating to hold all this power in check. But these were winding country lanes and that would have been crazy. The engine purred like a contented cat and Harriet was almost purring herself. 'Mmm,' she said, 'this is terrific!'

'What car do you have?'

'I'm between at the moment. My last was a Stag.'

'Why did you get rid of it?'

She would have said something about mechanical trouble or getting tired of that model. She shouldn't be driving any car, but they were only going into a not-very-busy market town, and she would only be behind the wheel for a few minutes. Nobody need know, and she was revelling in the fluid rushing motion, relaxing as swimming, exhilarating as dancing, when they rounded a bend and there, a little way ahead, was a partridge crossing the road.

The road was clear and running straight far enough for evasive action. Harriet swerved wide and missed the partridge, that rose in flapping flight, skimming the hedgerow, and landing in a field. There was no danger. She was in complete control of the car all the time, but that could have been a pedestrian, or a bike, or a car on the wrong side, and if she got involved in even the slightest accident she would be in bad trouble.

It brought home to her what a stupid risk she was taking,

and she drew up close to the grass verge and said, 'You'd better take over.'

'Are you all right?' he asked.

'Of course.' She was surprised to see her hand shaking slightly when she took it from the wheel. She felt a little lightheaded; perhaps she should have eaten some breakfast.

'Sit still,' said Jotham. She had turned to open her door and get out, and when he reached to hold her in her seat she strained away from him, but after a brief slight struggle she sat still. She needed to get her breath back. Her breath had caught when his hand closed on her arm, she was breathing shallowly now, and she would hate him to start wondering if he was disturbing her. He was looking at her as though something puzzled him.

She knew that she was pale, and she felt rather faint, she would certainly eat her lunch; and to stop his questions before they started she said, 'You had better take the wheel. I shouldn't have been driving—I don't have a licence.'

'I see.' He wasn't surprised. 'Why not?'

'Three speeding endorsements.'

He started up the car and she thought that perhaps they were going to drive the rest of the way in silence, that he was too exasperated to waste words on her, but he said shortly, 'You've no more sense than a spoiled child. You *are* a spoiled child.'

That I never was, she thought. She said, 'I know, it was stupid. I haven't driven before, not since I was banned. And I won't again.'

'Not in my property you won't,' he growled, and she flushed because it had been a lunatic thing to do. She wouldn't have been insured if she had damaged his car. 'It's such a beautiful car,' she pleaded, 'I wanted——'

'And what you want overrides every consideration,' he snapped.

That was roughly what Nigel had said about him, but Jotham Gaul would never do silly things, for no better reason than the moment's whim. Harriet tried to apologise. 'I'm sorry, I shouldn't——'

'Shut up, Beauty,' he said brusquely. 'I can stand looking at you, but I can't stand listening to you. You're an exceptionally thick young woman.'

If they hadn't been moving at a fair rate she would have jumped out of the car there and then. He had cause to be mad at her, she had behaved irresponsibly, but she was not thick, and it was all she could do to bite back a flood of angry words.

As soon as they did slow down she would be out. She'd walk or hitch, and when she did reach Mr Snelson's office she would tell him that a way had to be found to sell the works to somebody, anybody, who wasn't Jotham Gaul.

She kept her head turned, looking out of the car because she couldn't stand the sight of him. Damn him and his car —which of course she should not have been driving. She could have let herself in for a heavy fine, even a prison sentence. As her indignation subsided she had to admit that she had been thick, and scrambling out of the car and flouncing off would only make her look sillier.

So she stayed where she was, and not another word was spoken until Jotham Gaul parked beautifully right in front of the office in the main road. A car was just moving out, and Harriet sighed. She would have preferred him to have had to hunt for a parking space, driving round and round town, asking her to keep a watch out. It was very irritating when things went easily for him.

As she came round to the pavement she observed, 'I bet this always happens for you.'

'What?'

'This.' She nodded towards the car. 'A parking space.' He shook his head impatiently, she *was* talking nonsense, and she said, 'Thanks for the lift. Goodbye.'

'I'm coming in.' He locked his door and went round to check hers, and she said,

'Not with me.'

'I made an appointment for both of us,' he told her.

He must have phoned while she was getting into her coat and brushing her hair, and if she had felt stronger she would have told him, 'O.K., it's your appointment, and what are you and Mr Snelson going to natter about until I say I'll sell the factory?' But as she had to sell she wanted it over and done with.

A heavy door with a brass plate on it was secured back, and a swing door, glass-pannelled, led from the small porch. She pushed the swing door and found it resistant, hard to shove, and Jotham leaned over her and pushed it wide.

I'm weak as water, she thought. Maybe I don't really want to walk in here, and see Mr Snelson and arrange for the sale. Maybe I didn't want that door to open. She knew for sure that the towering form of Jotham Gaul behind her was making her nervous.

They stepped into an office and four women looked up, two from typewriters. Harriet was used to wistful faces as women assessed her at first sight, followed by anything from smiles to looks that could kill. But this time she only got a passing glance; all four women were smiling at Jotham, and the one who said, 'Can I help you?' asked him, not Harriet.

Mr Snelson came round his desk to greet them as they were ushered into his room, and shook them both warmly by the hand. He was pleased to see them here together. The sooner Jotham Gaul took over the factory the better it would be for everybody, including Harriet, and when Gaul had phoned half an hour ago Mr Snelson had promptly cancelled a previous appointment.

'Well now,' he said jovially, when everyone was seated, 'I presume this means you've been talking things over?'

'Well, yes,' said Harriet, 'certainly we've been talking things over. We've done a lot of talking since we bumped into each other again yesterday.' She was seized with an upsurge of mischief, staring coolly at Jotham Gaul. 'But not about business. We haven't gone too deeply into your actual business matters, have we? Except that I seem to remember saying I'd rather burn the place down than sell it to you.'

Mr Snelson blinked rapidly and Joth said, 'Risky business, arson. I know you don't think the laws of the land apply to you, but that would be going a bit far.'

Mr Snelson decided they were joking, Joth was grinning, and he asked Harriet, 'You have decided to sell?' She shrugged and he took that as meaning yes. 'Mr Gaul has told you his offer?'

'No,' she said, 'except that I wouldn't get a better.'

The accountant didn't believe she would. He began to talk and Harriet tried to listen. He went on and on, level-toned, no emphasis on anything, a dry statement of facts and figures. A hum of traffic rose from the street below and sometimes a phone rang. He mentioned names she knew, men who helped run the works, her father's solicitors, and she wondered if they would protect her interests, if she could trust them. She felt sure enough about Mr Snelson, and in any case she couldn't have carried on running the factory. That was another impossible dream. She knew nothing about the business world.

'Would you like to go along to the works?' Mr Snelson was asking her, and she said firmly,

'No, thank you.'

'I was there yesterday afternoon.' He was opening a drawer in his desk. 'I brought this back for you. It stood on your father's desk.'

He handed her her mother's photograph in the silver frame and she stared at it until he said, 'It's your *mother*.'

'Of course it is.' She had a cloud of fair hair, and the studio picture made her mouth softly luminous, her eyes very clear and direct, grey liner and mascara and shadow make-up emphasising them.

Every time she had looked straight at Harriet her glance had slid away, like those women in the office just now, to something more interesting. Harriet almost expected the photograph to do that now, she had never held her mother's scrutiny before. She shivered and said, 'I don't remember her very well. I didn't see much of her.'

She didn't tell them that she had no happy memories so far as her mother was concerned, and when neither man spoke she put the photograph flat on the desk and said, 'There isn't much I can do here, is there? Will you get in touch with the lawyers for me, and see if we can get a better offer than Mr Gaul's? If not——' she shrugged and Mr Snelson said,

'I will do that.' Harriet was still looking pale. His wife had said she didn't eat enough to keep a bird alive. These modern girls, he thought, and was almost glad that he had no children of his own.

'Do you think you could find me a carrier bag?' Harriet asked.

He touched a bell and a few minutes later she left the office with her mother's photograph in the plastic Mothercare bag provided by one of the girls in the outer office.

She went into a café with flat bow windows and homemade cakes, and fresh sandwiches, and sat near a window with a cup of coffee and a toasted teacake, watching the people go by. She wasn't hungry. The teacake stuck in her throat, and nobody who went by seemed to be alone. Except the women with bags and baskets, obviously shopping for their families.

Her mother's photograph had made her feel lonelier than ever. Tomorrow she would go back to London and her flat and Anthony. No, not Anthony, but she did have friends who would be glad to see her.

She left most of the teacake on her plate and bought a doughnut and a cheese and tomato sandwich when she paid the bill. She thought she might go down to the river and eat them later, but first she wandered up and down the high street, peering into every window. Some of the shops were attractive enough, but none was anywhere near London standards, and the dress shops had nothing that tempted her to step inside.

She looked in the antique shops, with some idea of buying herself a present to cheer herself up, but there was nothing she wanted to live with.

She got plenty of looks from passers-by and didn't notice any of them any more than she felt the shadows of the almond trees falling across her shoulders.

After a while she went down to the river. She hadn't been down there for years, but nothing had changed. There was the boathouse where punts and small motorboats were hired out. Visitors strolled around, young children played on the grass along the towpath watched over by young mothers, retired locals sat on their usual benches chatting and sunning themselves.

It was a lovely day and Harriet walked a little way, then sat down on a bench that circled a huge old cedar and broke up her doughnut and scattered it to the ducks that waddled up the river bank. She skimmed some into the water, followed by the sandwich, and the slight exertion made her head swim.

Suppose she was really ill, who would look after her? Her friends, of course, but she didn't need looking after because she knew what the matter was. She hadn't felt hungry since her father had died and she hadn't bothered, and that was stupid.

She closed her eyes now, leaning back with the sun on her face, feeling relaxed and drowsy. A little rest would help, and then she would walk back into town and get a taxi. She might go to the Snelsons; Mrs Snelson wouldn't mind. But her cases were at Tudor House, she would be leaving from there in the morning, so it might be less trouble to go back to Tudor House.

She slipped into a light doze and as easily slipped out of it when someone sat down beside her. A girl, wearing jeans and a pink cheesecloth shirt, with one hand on a pushchair containing a sleeping baby and a hook-on basket full of groceries, smiled and said, 'Hello.'

'Hello,' Harriet echoed.

'Lovely weather, isn't it?'

'Isn't it?'

'I get as far as here,' said the girl, 'then I flop for five minutes.' Her face was shining with perspiration and she blew from an underlip lifting her fringe slightly. She had been shopping in the town and the towpath took her to a little new estate. She started talking, about the terrible price of everything, what that basket of food had totted up to, and Harriet nodded, agreeing, and admired the sleeping baby.

'He's beautiful. What's his name?'

'William,' said his mother proudly, 'and he's a terror.' She looked at Harriet with the familiar puzzled half-recognition. 'Do I—should I know you? I mean—haven't I seen you somewhere?'

'I've been in a few magazines,' said Harriet, and the girl's face cleared.

'Oh *yes*!' she wanted to hear all about the glamour of modelling and Harriet tried to answer her questions, and she would have stayed for hours if Harriet hadn't glanced at her watch and said, 'I'll have to be going.'

'Me too,' said the girl, and grimaced, 'My old man'll be waiting for his tea. It was lovely meeting you. Aren't you lucky?'

'Am I?' Harriet hadn't questioned that for a long time. She wouldn't have questioned it now if she had felt healthier, and the girl, who was nice and friendly and ordinary, said,

'With your looks you are just about the luckiest girl I've ever seen.'

Harriet laughed, 'You should catch me first thing in the morning!' and the girl laughed too, hoping it was true that there were times when the born knock-outs looked much as she did herself.

She went off, pushing her baby and the groceries, and Harriet walked back along the towpath towards the town. The girl was the lucky one, Harriet thought. There was somebody waiting for her. There was nobody, anywhere in the world, waiting for Harriet.

CHAPTER FOUR

No one answered when Harriet knocked on the door of Tudor House. The taxi had just left and there seemed to be no one around the front of the house. But this was a working farm, unlikely to be deserted mid-afternoon. Around the back there would surely be someone in the outhouses or just across the fields.

She lifted the heavy brass ring of the knocker again and the door moved slightly; she pushed it open and called, 'Anyone home?'

Nobody came. She walked across the hall and up the stairs and called, 'Hello!' on the gallery. Then she went to her room. Funny, thinking of it as 'her' room when, after tomorrow, she would never sleep in here again. But this afternoon was like coming home.

She had come quietly along this corridor, and she hadn't called any more 'Hello's'. Jotham might be in his room and, as usual, he was the last person she wanted to meet. She dropped her coat on a chair and kicked off her shoes. She was still tired. If the girl with the pram hadn't sat down beside her she would have dozed on, in the sunshine, by the river. Now she stretched out on top of the bed and sank into its downy softness, thinking of nothing, making her mind a blank and letting the peace flow in.

When she woke she was surprised to find that she had slept for the best part of three hours. She *must* have been exhausted; handing over the works to Jotham Gaul had taken its toll. Nigel should be home by now, soon anyway, and she did a light make-up repair job, lips and eyes and blusher, then started brushing her hair.

She grinned at herself in the mirror, with her hair over one eye. 'Oh, you're worth coming home to,' she said. 'You're looking very good tonight.'

Then the grin faded because no one was coming home to her, and she didn't feel good, she felt rotten. When she jerked her head the room shimmered, and she knew she had to start getting some food down her. She didn't feel like eating, but she didn't feel like making herself ill either.

Downstairs in the hall she called again 'Hello!' and Nigel came hurrying out, beaming a welcome, hands outstretched.

'Hello, where have you been? Where did you come from?'

'Up there,' she said.

'We didn't know you were here. I've been ringing around. Mother thought you might have gone back to London.'

'And left my cases?' She smiled. 'Tomorrow,' she said. Nigel looked ready to argue, then changed his mind and took her into a room where the evening meal was being eaten. Jotham and Mrs Joliffe sat at the table, with steaks on their plates, and Harriet felt squeamish. She might have managed a little soup, or one of the side salads, but not a great hunk of meat.

She sat in a chair next to Nigel's. A place had been laid here, and she was glad to sit down. 'Everything settled, then?' she asked Jotham.

'Hardly,' he said, 'but soon, I hope.'

'Have you eaten?' Nigel wanted to know, and she shook her head. 'Not all day?' His voice rose. 'And you had no breakfast, did you?' He sounded anxious about her and Mrs Joliffe said brightly,

'Joth says Mr Snelson had your mother's photograph for you. I remember her, of course.'

She was trying to break up the moment of intimacy

between Nigel and Harriet, and she succeeded, because they stopped looking at each other and looked at her, and she went on, 'She was very beautiful.'

'May I see it?' asked Nigel, and Harriet gasped,

'I left it! The photograph—by a bench, by the river.'

'That was very absentminded,' Jotham drawled, and Mrs Joliffe said,

'You *never*! However did you come to do that?' as though this was one of the most extraordinary things she had ever heard; and it did sound heartless, Harriet walking off and leaving the photograph of her mother that her father had cherished. Well, she had. And she'd never thought about it again until now.

She tried to explain, 'I—didn't feel too good. I got a taxi and came back here, and as soon as I got back I fell asleep, and I just forgot it.'

'Hadn't you better go back and see if it's still there?' said Jotham.

'I suppose so, yes.' Her head was spinning, and so were her thoughts. She didn't think the blue and white carrier bag would be where she'd left it nearly four hours ago. It was quite conspicuous. If someone had picked it up they might have handed it in. But the silver frame was valuable, so it might not have been handed in. Then again it might not have been touched. Unattended packages often got a wide berth these days, pointed out to the police by passers-by who then stood well back to wait for the bomb disposal squad.

'Shall I take you?' Nigel was asking her, and she tried to stand up and the room began to swim around her, and she felt herself slithering down in her chair while Nigel went on calling her name, faint and faraway.

'Harriet'—her name was getting clearer, and she was coming back. She was in one of the big armchairs now, head ridiculously down between her knees. As she shuddered and gasped she was gently eased upright, head back on a cushion.

She must have fainted. She had never fainted before and it was a ghastly sensation. She could feel clammy cold sweat on her brow and nausea churning in her stomach. Her hair fell over her face and Nigel smoothed it back with a tender touch, muttering about calling a doctor.

She protested, 'It isn't necessary, I'm all right.' She ran the tip of her tongue between her dry lips, her voice had sounded cracked, then she said, 'I've been a bit of an idiot. Since my father died I've been missing meals and that sort of thing. It caught up on me today.'

'I told you you needed taking care of.' Nigel was rubbing her hands and she was shivering, and she smiled because it was nice to be comforted. Even Mrs Joliffe, also bending over her, seemed concerned.

But Jotham Gaul was not. He stood well back and she could read his thoughts. He felt she could take very good care of herself. He was suspicious that her black-out was an act put on for sympathy, and she said huskily, 'Do I need looking after?' as much to annoy him as to please Nigel, who chimed in eagerly,

'And you need a holiday.'

Harriet was recovering fast. She did her upwards look through fluttering eyelashes. 'Where shall we go?' and was a little taken aback when Nigel said promptly, 'How about a villa on an island just off Sicily? Joth has one, and a few of us are going over next month for an annual *festa*. You could come. Why don't you?'

She didn't look at Joth and his silence was hardly encouraging. 'It sounds wonderful' she said to Nigel, 'but what does Joth have to say to this invitation?' and then she looked at Joth.

He didn't want her in his villa, he didn't want her anywhere near him, and his voice was gentle and soft and chilly. 'Be my guest,' he said, and she might have been wise to say, 'No, thank you,' because she wouldn't get much hospitality from that host. But she hated to do anything he wanted her to do, and if she went on this holiday it would mean a little time with Nigel, a chance to get to know him better.

She would like that, and she had no other immediate plans. 'Thank you,' she said sweetly, 'I'd love to,' and had the satisfaction of seeing Jotham Gaul's expression become even grimmer.

'What about Annie?' Sylvia Joliffe asked plaintively. Annie was going on this holiday, Annie who was the right girl for Nigel in his mother's opinion, and she could have shaken her son for being so blind.

He said now, not taking his eyes off Harriet, 'It's a big villa, there's room,' as though the only worry was whether there would be enough beds.

'There'll always be room for Annie,' said Joth, and Sylvia darted him a glance of entreaty. 'Aren't you going back to look for your mother's photograph?' asked Joth, and Nigel protested,

'Have a heart! Give her a minute. She's going to eat something. Can't you see the girl's been neglecting herself?'

'She's always looked that way,' said Jotham. 'Every time I've seen her. Hungry.'

'Anything will do,' said Harriet.

'I'll see to your steak.' Sylvia turned with her martyred air, and Harriet said,

'Please, I couldn't eat a steak.'

'Not that hungry?' said Jotham. 'How about a nice glass of hot milk?' He was being sarcastic, treating her like an invalid, and it was just bad luck that he had struck one of her real hates.

'No, thank you,' she said. 'Could I have some soup, per-

haps?' The cutlery in her place at the table had included
a soup spoon, and now Nigel was on his way to the door.

'Can you make it back to the table?' Josh enquired soli-
citously. 'Or shall we serve you where you are?'

Harriet got up at that. Sylvia Joliffe followed her son—
probably, thought Harriet, to ask him what he imagined
was going to happen with both Harriet and Annie holiday-
ing in the villa—and Jotham Gaul watched Harriet steadily.

She got back to her chair at the table. She wouldn't
have stumbled for worlds. He might have caught her if she
had, and that would have made her flesh creep. More likely
he would have let her fall flat on her face, because he didn't
believe she had fainted in the first place. It was hard for
her to believe herself. It was only when she thought back
on how many meals she must have skipped this last week
that it stopped being surprising.

Joth sat down. She wondered why he was at the head
of the table, in the carver chair, when he was only a lodger
in the house. Nigel should be in there. But Joth was the
bigger man, so they put him in the bigger chair. Of course
there was no other method in the order of seating. She
was still a little lightheaded and it niggled her to see him
at the head of the table. He'd take over anywhere, she
thought. Give him any table, dining room, boardroom, and
he'd seat himself at the top.

'Stop glowering at me,' he said, 'you're getting frown
lines.' Instinctively her forefinger fled to the furrowed
spot between her brows and he grinned. 'That's right,
smooth it away, we can't be doing with wrinkles.'

'*We* can't?' She sniffed. 'You'll have to. You couldn't
smooth your face with a steam iron!'

'How true.' He agreed with that. 'You're very sharp for
a girl who's faint from malnutrition.'

Whether he believed it or not that was exactly what she
was, weak because she hadn't eaten, so she took a bread

roll, broke off a little and put it in her mouth. She needed to build up her strength. She had an enemy here who was a constant challenge. She said, chewing on the dry bread, 'A holiday in Sicily will set me up. How kind of you to invite me.'

'You think so?' He looked at her with a slight smile, eyes under heavy lids searching her face. 'Perhaps it was. If you come along with Nigel and Annie I'll take good care of you.'

Harriet didn't care to meet his eyes and she found herself looking at his hands and thinking how powerful they were. 'Take care of you' when he said it had a sinister sound.

Nigel brought a bowl of steaming soup and set it in front of her. It was a pale creamy green and tasted of leeks and potatoes, probably home-made by his mother who sat down again, and picked up her knife and fork and said to Nigel, 'Your meal's spoiling.'

'I'll go and see if I can find your photograph. Where exactly did you leave it?' Nigel asked Harriet, and the more Harriet protested that he should finish his dinner first the more determined he became. He was anxious to do something for her by retrieving her mother's picture.

'Over the bridge, past the boathouse,' she said at last. 'About five minutes along the towpath there's a big cedar tree. I sat down on the bench under that and I put the carrier bag on the ground beside me. I suppose it could have got knocked under the seat.'

'A blue and white bag,' Jotham interposed.

'If it isn't there I'll ask around,' said Nigel. 'Don't worry, nobody's likely to pinch a photograph.'

'This one was in a heavy silver frame,' said Jotham, and Sylvia tutted because this made Harriet doubly careless.

Nigel admitted that a silver frame reduced his chances of getting the photograph back, but he gave Harriet a quick kiss on the cheek and said he'd get along and see, and she said, 'You are kind going to all this trouble,' and he said it was nothing.

As they heard his car start his mother picked up his plate and said crossly, 'I'll take this into the kitchen and try to keep it warm.' She thought it was Harriet's fault. Nigel was being foolish, but Harriet had been quite heartless, leaving her mother's photograph under a bench on the river bank and not bothering about it at all.

Harriet put down her spoon. She hadn't wanted to disrupt their meal and upset everybody. She wished she'd had her mind on her bag when she'd walked away and not on the girl she had been talking to, and not feeling groggy.

'Can't you manage it?' Joth enquired. 'Do you need feeding?'

'Don't be ridiculous,' she said shortly, 'although forcefeeding might be in your line.' She went back to the soup, starting to eat again, and he asked,

'Do you think he'll find it?'

'I don't know.'

'Do you care?'

'Of course I care!' But if she had cared she wouldn't have left it. Jotham wasn't eating, he was watching her, and she raised her eyes and met his in a level unflinching gaze. 'No,' she said, 'not much. She never cared for me. When I was a kid I was too plain to be a credit to either of them.'

His heavy brows raised at that and she went on, 'Were you poor before you were rich?'

'Yes,' he said.

'How many friends did you have then?'

'A few.'

'Lucky you! When I was plain I had no friends, and every time my mother looked at me she sighed.' He was expressionless and she went on, 'Well, that's how it seemed.

I don't think I meant to leave that photograph behind, but a psychiatrist might say different, and if it does turn up again I won't be hanging it on my wall because it would give me no joy. Does that answer your question?'

'Very fully.' After a moment he said, 'Another question?'

'Why not?'

'Are you playing for sympathy? First the faint, then the sob story.' Her spine was stiff, she was taut as a bow already, so nothing he said was likely to make her flinch.

'No,' she snapped back. 'I don't want sympathy. You asked me whether I cared if the photograph was found and I told you. And nobody was more surprised than I was when I fainted. Although you think it was an act.'

'It had crossed my mind,' he said gravely. 'Malnutrition seemed unlikely. Are you pregnant, by any chance?'

'By no chance.' When she had finished her soup she might throw the bowl at him. She raised her beautifully arched eyebrows, trying to look as though this was rather amusing. 'Is that why you think I might let Nigel look after me? What a sweet old-fashioned idea!'

'It is rather.'

'No,' she said. 'No. But I will tell you something that might come as a surprise to you. Until you and his mother started talking about marriage I wasn't looking for a husband—I could soon have found one if I had been. But I'm getting fonder of Nigel all the time, and right now I'm coming round to the idea that I might like to marry him. You put that idea in my head, and you made another mistake when you said he wouldn't want to marry me. So thank you again for inviting me to the villa where Nigel and I can really get to know each other.'

She was talking more than she should, but at least she was giving as good as she got. Jotham had listened with what seemed to be polite attention, but there was some-

thing very-rough, very tough about him, although he
grinned when he said, 'I should have thought that was
the last thing you'd have wanted. He's more likely to stay
infatuated if he doesn't know what you're like inside the
body beautiful.'

Harriet laughed. 'As you said earlier—with me the body
beautiful is all. How's Annie for looks? I'm considered
pretty devastating in a bikini.'

'I'm sure you are.' She couldn't have explained why
she suddenly half turned away, with folded arms as though
she was covering nakedness. Nor why her face grew suddenly hot. Then he grinned. 'Somebody should warn the
sharks you're coming,' he said.

The return of Sylvia Joliffe stopped the talking. From
then on an uncomfortable silence reigned. She took her
place again and went on with her meal, and everything
about her was disapproving, from the quivering set of her
shoulders to the clatter of her knife and fork.

She was annoyed that Nigel had gone dashing off to
look for something that shouldn't have been lost in the
first place; and she was bitterly opposed to the idea of
Harriet joining the young folk in Joth's villa.

Joth could hardly have refused to let her, but Sylvia
Joliffe hoped that somehow he would manage things so
that Annie wasn't humiliated and Nigel would be brought
back to his senses. Joth had always been something of a
miracle worker. Sylvia Joliffe had a lot of faith in Jotham
Gaul.

Joth was not contributing anything to the conversation
around this table. He said nothing, and Harriet's attempts
got a chilly response. She tried to apologise, 'I'm sorry
about this. I do wish Nigel had waited to finish his meal
first.'

'So do I,' snapped his mother.

A little while later Harriet said, 'I spent the morning in

Upper Camden. It is a pretty town isn't it? I went into a little café called The Cobweb.'

'I thought you said you hadn't eaten' said Nigel's mother and Harriet tried to explain,

'I didn't really. I ordered something but I didn't eat it.'

'Do you want any more soup?' The offer was grudging, every word that Sylvia Joliffe spoke to her was grudging, and Harriet wondered if she could ever break through this woman's prejudice. If the time should come when she might badly want Sylvia Joliffe to like or at least to tolerate her.

She declined the soup, but when the dessert of fruit, cheese and apple pie came in, she took an apple, and peeled and ate that.

By now Joth and Sylvia were talking to each other, about property being built at the other end of the village, excluding Harriet as though she wasn't there. It wasn't just bad manners. It was a deliberate policy to shut her out, and she cut her apple segments into smaller pieces and played around with them on her plate, and smiled when she heard a car that sounded like Nigel's coming closer.

They were riling her so badly that she was in two minds whether to jump up, and fling her arms around him and kiss him soundly, as soon as he came into the room. But she didn't. She didn't want things moving that fast with Nigel, and besides, Jotham was waiting for her to do something that would show they had upset her.

It was better to stay cool and smiling, and Nigel's crestfallen expression showed that his trip had been unsuccessful before he said a word.

'Never mind,' Harriet said impulsively, 'it doesn't matter.'

He sounded frustrated and fed up. 'No sign of it. I rang the police and nobody seems to have handed it in. I'll ring up the boatyard in the morning.' He came and sat down beside her while his mother tutted again and went out to fetch his dinner.

'Thank you anyway,' said Harriet, and she stroked his unhappy face, 'I've got other photographs of her.' She hadn't, but there were several in her father's apartment, and as she had told Jotham, her mother's photograph was almost like that of a stranger.

She couldn't say that to Nigel, but probably Jotham would tell him. She would have to watch that Jotham didn't rattle her into saying things she didn't want repeating. She wanted Nigel to think well of her, but Jotham brought out the worst.

'That doesn't look very appetising,' said Sylvia Joliffe, banging down the dinner plate, reminding Harriet of the wasted breakfast bacon.

'Nothing wrong with it,' said Nigel, and ate some. But it had dried up, and he turned to a slice of apple pie. 'Has Joth been telling you about the villa?' he asked Harriet.

If he imagined that Jotham Gaul had been entertaining Harriet with glowing accounts of his holiday island he had the wrong picture. 'No,' she said sweetly, 'except that there are sharks about.'

'Very rarely.' Nigel was anxious she shouldn't be scared into staying with him. 'But there are sometimes dolphins.'

'Lovely,' said Harriet. 'I hope somebody will warn the dolphins I'm on my way.'

Nigel chuckled, 'Tell them they've a treat in store? Do you like swimming?'

'Yes, I do.' She was a strong swimmer.

'It's a wonderful beach. White sand and marvellously clear water. And the villa's something, isn't it?' he appealed to Jotham, and Jotham nodded. 'A bit run down now,' Nigel went on enthusiastically, 'but it's been splendid. It always belonged to the same family, didn't it?' Again

Jotham nodded. 'Then they died out all except a distant relation who didn't want it and Joth bought it last summer.'

'A run-down villa last summer,' Harriet murmured, 'A run-down factory this. Will you give them both the kiss of life?'

'That's the idea,' said Joth.

'Most of the island goes with the villa,' said Nigel. 'It's going to be a holiday development.'

'A profitable investment, of course,' muttered Harriet.

'Of course,' said Joth.

'It's something, I tell you,' Nigel told Harriet. 'It's an extraordinary place, out of this world—Piccola Licata. You know Sicily?'

She said, 'Yes.' She hadn't been there, but she knew where it was, and that was what he meant.

'Well, Piccola Licata is in the Gulf of Gela, about ten miles off shore. We fly to Palermo and it's a couple of days from there.'

'When?' Harriet asked.

'The fifth of next month. 'Can you manage that?' He waited anxiously. That was in two weeks' time, and he was afraid the notice was too short.

'I'm sure I can.'

'You don't have any commitments?' That was Joth, of course. 'No modelling engagements?'

'Not at the moment.'

'Lady of leisure?'

'For the next few weeks, yes.'

'And what are your plans, then?' As she had just told him she could be considering Nigel as a husband he knew very well what her plans were. Getting to know Nigel better and seeing what happened from there. She said, 'I don't believe in planning too far ahead. You never know what's going to happen. Things have changed a great deal for me in the past two weeks.'

She had lost her father and perhaps she had found Nigel. She hoped she had found the man she would fall in love with. She needed love. She needed a man she could trust.

'How true,' said Jotham.

'What is?'

'That you never know what's going to happen,' he said, and a shiver ran down her spine.

She really didn't feel up to going out that evening and when they sat down together in the drawing room Jotham made three. He was very good company, so far as an intruder could be. Harriet could have done without him, and she was sure that Nigel would rather have been alone with her, but Jotham talked about the villa and the island and it was enthralling stuff.

Anyone would have believed he was glad Harriet was joining them. Nigel was fooled, chiming in with little bits of description, adding to Jotham's glowing account of the place.

Harriet knew Jotham was here to stop Nigel doing something rash and committing like kissing her, or telling her he was crazy about her, or asking if he could come to her room later. She would have said 'No' to a midnight visit, but Jotham wasn't to know that, and he was going to have his work cut out if he intended to keep them apart permanently. Anyhow, what business was it of his? Except that he considered himself part of the Joliffe family, Sylvia was his mother figure, Nigel was nearly a brother; and of course he had a king-sized contempt for Harriet.

There had been a natural antipathy between them from the beginning and now there was a little war. She did want to go on this holiday and really get to know Nigel, but she also wanted to win against Jotham. She sat beside Nigel and listened to the men talking about Piccola Licata and the old villa and ruins of the little Roman temple, and it sounded a spellbinding place.

Her eyes widened, glowing and green, and she said, 'I can't wait to see it.'

'You'll have a super holiday,' Nigel assured her. 'We've been over several times. Marvellous!'

'Yes,' said Jotham softly, 'I guarantee that your stay in my villa will be unforgettable,' and Nigel smiled. But both Harriet and Jotham knew that the memories Harriet was being promised were the kind she would want to forget.

CHAPTER FIVE

NEXT day Harriet went to her father's apartment as soon as she had left her luggage in her own flat. She could have found a friend to go with her, but she wasn't sure how she was going to react. She hadn't been in here since news came of her father's death, and if she should break down she would rather nobody saw her.

It was a very desirable residence, overlooking Primrose Hill and Regents Park. With a lease of only four years to run it would still bring in a fair sum and obviously she had to sell. But first she had to sort out personal possessions.

There was a stark tidiness about the rooms. The girl who ran the art gallery and her husband had been in while Harriet was away, moving things that made the apartment look as though Henry Brookes might be coming back, clearing toilet articles, taking away magazines and paperbacks, putting all clothes and shoes in cupboards and drawers.

Harriet packed family photographs, two of her mother, one of her father, and one of herself taken about twelve months ago, in the small suitcase she had brought with her. She put the more personal items on the big polished Regency table in the window. Her father had had friends who might like something that had belonged to him. Out of these she packed a silver cigarette case. He had given up smoking cigarettes years ago, ever since the health scare started, but when she was a child he had carried that with him everywhere.

Then she went to the desk to start through the papers and her eyes blurred at the sight of her father's handwrit-

ing. She blinked hard and was thankful the drawers weren't
too full.

Henry Brookes was not a man who kept old correspon-
dence; everything was current. There were personal letters
she tore up with a wry smile, he had always been successful with the ladies. Accounts, mostly unpaid. Bank statements.

She wasn't surprised to find the bank statements were
heavily in the red. She found herself smiling again, shaking her head and thinking—but of course, with the bills
outstanding that's the apartment and the furniture spoken
for; and then she went on with her task.

Night was falling when she finished. She sat for a little
while, in the dusk, in a chair by the table with the telephone on it. Soon she would go out and get a tube or a
taxi to friends who would comfort her. But she wished
there was somebody whose number she could dial, and just
say, 'Please come.'

She could walk out of here alone, she always had walked
alone. But tonight she ached for someone to come when
she called, because he loved her so much that she could
break down and cry in his arms, and he wouldn't care if she
looked ugly from weeping. Or when she grew old and the
wrinkles came.

Perhaps, one day, Nigel might feel like that about her,
if Jotham Gaul gave them a chance. The thought of Jotham
got her on her feet and held back the tears. She wanted
to think of Nigel, there was some comfort in that, but
she couldn't get Jotham Gaul out of her mind. Every time
she thought of Nigel she thought of Jotham too, and that
wasn't comforting at all.

Dorothy McGill lived with her husband above the little
gallery that Harriet helped to finance just off Twickenham
Green. They sold paintings and sculpture at reasonable
prices, and most months put on exhibitions of what they

hoped were up-and-coming artists. This month the paintings looked angry, splashes of raw clawing colour that
made Harriet wince. Daylight lighting in the window
showed a couple of them sharp and clear, and as she got
out of the taxi and pushed the bell she thought—Jotham
Gaul would wear a shirt in that pattern.

Dorothy came down to open the door, a plumpish very
pretty girl with energy and drive. She hadn't wanted callers,
they were just sitting down to their evening meal, but she
smiled when she saw Harriet. Harriet came here and slept
in their spare room whenever she felt like it, just as she
helped on the sales side when she had time on her hands.
'When did you get back?' Dorothy asked as soon as she'd
said, 'Hello, come on in.'

'Today. I've just come from my father's apartment.'

'Did you go there on your own?' Dorothy threw a
slightly anxious look over her shoulder, leading the way
upstairs.

'Yes.' That couldn't have been too good for her, Dorothy thought, and Harriet was looking tired now. 'Thanks
for going round, you and Sam,' said Harriet. 'It made it
easier, the clutter being gone.'

Sam got up and kissed her the way Dorothy had at the
door, quietly welcoming. Since her father had died Dorothy
and Sam had felt really sorry for her. Nobody had ever
felt sorry for her before. They had thought she had everything, and this was the first cloud in her life since her
mother's death. 'She's been round to the apartment,' said
Dorothy, and Sam took off Harriet's coat and drew up
another chair to the table.

'Sit down,' he said. 'Is there any more of this?'

'This' was casseroled chops and there wasn't, so Harriet
said, 'Can I go and find something in the kitchen?'

She knew Dorothy's kitchen as well as her own. While
they went back to their meal she made herself a thick

chutney and ham sandwich, and Dorothy laughed when she came back with it. 'Your appetite's taken a turn for the better.'

'I've got to keep my strength up.' Harriet bit into the sandwich. 'I'm broke,' she said. 'The factory's being sold, it seems it's been running down for ages. All my father left are debts.' She took another bite while they looked at each other, each hoping the other would say something.

They'd believed her father was a wealthy man. Harriet had never seemed to bother about money, and Dorothy said, 'But *you're* not broke, there's your modelling.'

'I was thinking of something more regular. I thought they might find me something in the factory, but the man who's taking that over wouldn't give me a job there sweeping up.' She chewed on. She had overdone the size of this sandwich, it was taking some swallowing.

Dorothy said suddenly, 'If you're serious about a full-time job you could work here—you're a very good saleswoman.'

'Am I?' Harriet helped here for fun, not seriously, but she did enjoy selling.

'You've got an eye for layout too,' Dorothy went on. 'Hanging the exhibitions.'

'Have I?' She hadn't thought she had anything, except her looks, and Dorothy was probably just being kind, offering her a job. But it was an idea, it was something to think about. She said, 'Thank you. Look, I'm going on holiday in a fortnight for a couple of weeks. I met this man I used to know, at the funeral, actually, and I'm going with him and some others to a villa on an island off Sicily, and a lot depends on how well we get on together. I mean, I might not come back here to live.'

Sam smiled, 'Oh ho!'

'This bit's in confidence,' said Harriet, 'but if he asks me I could marry him.'

She might, if he did. If Jotham Gaul didn't spoil it all,
and somehow make Nigel turn away from her and back
to Annie whatever-her-name was. This holiday was going
to be overshadowed by Jotham.

'Is he rich?' asked Dorothy.

'Filthy rich,' snapped Harriet, then, 'No—no, he isn't.
He has a farm and a lovely old Tudor house, but he's far
from being rich.'

Dorothy and Sam looked puzzled, as well they might,
and Harriet could hardly explain that she had answered
automatically, talking about another man ...

Nigel rang every evening, and they talked about what
they had done that day. Mostly what he had done. She
liked to hear what was going on in and around Tudor
House, it was almost like being there, and as the holiday
came nearer she found that she was looking forward to
seeing him again, almost as much as he said he was longing
to see her.

They were all meeting at Heathrow. Nigel apologised that
he couldn't meet her ahead, alone. He was driving Annie
up, that had been arranged ages ago.

Annie was still coming to the island, but she knew that
Nigel had a new girl-friend who had been an old girl-
friend, and Harriet had to admit that showed courage.
Or perhaps it showed that Annie cared less for Nigel than
his mother had imagined. Harriet hoped she didn't care
too much, and wouldn't be hurt. She also hoped that she
wouldn't like Annie.

They were waiting when she arrived. She saw Nigel
first, because he was looking out for her where the taxis
drew up. He held her at arm's length, stared at her as
though she was something out of a dream, and exclaimed,
'You look fantastic.'

She was wearing a black silk shantung jacket, white
jersey silk T-shirt, matt black jersey trousers, and high-

heeled strap sandals. Her only jewellery was a slim ivory heart swinging on a long thin silver chain and silver earrings the shape and size of a pin's head. The effect was simple and dramatic. The flame of her hair and her tall lithe figure made people look at her, and her model-girl face kept them looking. Nigel was proud to take her arm, and see to her luggage, and conduct her up the stairs to meet the others.

He ushered her towards a man and two girls who were sitting drinking coffee, saying, 'There they are,' and Harriet felt she could pick out Annie even from this distance. Both girls were fair, one with softly waving hair, the other with a tossing tangle of curls. The one with the curls was the prettier, glaring at Harriet across the airport lounge, and having a hard time pretending to smile when they were face to face and Nigel was introducing her. 'This is Erica,' he said.

That shook Harriet, because surely Annie was the one with the grievance. Later she realised it was the old story— Erica was something of a glamour girl herself and she disliked the competition Harriet provided.

Annie was a small girl, and nothing much to look at until she smiled. Her smile was quick and shy and endearing. When she said, 'Hello,' and smiled Harriet could see why Nigel's mother thought she would make a good wife and daughter-in-law, and she wished that Erica had been her rival because Erica seemed a less likeable girl.

Alistair Wilson was the architect who would probably be working on the holiday development on Piccola Licata. He was in his early thirties, dark-haired and with a thin dark moustache, a dapper smiling man, married to the sulky Erica.

There was no sign of Jotham. Harriet had been steeling herself to face him again. After she had shaken hands all round and exchanged a few words she queried, 'No

Jotham?' and then she was told he would be meeting them on the island, that he had been in Milan for the past week.

Nigel hadn't mentioned that in their phone calls, Nigel hadn't mentioned Jotham at all, and she hadn't brought up his name because he was the last thing she wanted to talk about. 'Good,' she said now, with a broad relieved smile, delighted to hear that he wouldn't be breathing down the back of her neck during the three-day journey to the Gulf of Licata.

'Don't you like Jotham?' asked Erica, with what was almost certainly mock innocence, and Harriet went on smiling.

'That,' she said, 'is another story.'

The trip was pleasant. Harriet was a good traveller, she took little inconveniences in her stride, and all the arrangements went very smoothly. They stayed a night in Palermo, and crossed Sicily—staying another night en route—in a hired car, Alistair doing most of the driving.

She was never alone with Nigel and she must have seemed a little aloof to her fellow passengers. They knew each other well, they joked together, but she preferred to be left to her own thoughts, although most of the time she could feel Nigel's admiring eyes on her. Alistair's too, occasionally, when Erica was looking away.

The days since her father's death had been a continual strain, but now she was relaxed. It was almost like a time of convalescence, and she made no effort to become one of the group; so it was ridiculous that Nigel was becoming more and more infatuated with her. They had done no real talking at all. All they had shared had been seats on a plane and a car, hotel meals and separate rooms.

Nigel thought she was wonderful because she was striking to look at. He didn't know her at all, but she knew that he was pleasant and kind—except where poor little Annie was concerned, of course—and when they reached the

island it would be time, Harriet told herself, to decide
what her own feelings were for Nigel ...

A fishing boat was waiting to take them the ten miles
to Piccola Licata, and the island reared up out of a shining
sea. A volcano, extinct, everyone said, with olive groves and
orange and lemon orchards on its lower slopes and Harriet
took off her dark glasses to try to see better.

The sun's rays made the whole island seem a blaze
of light, shooting up from the glittering white beaches,
and obscuring the stark outline of the rocks, dazzling her
so that she quickly put on her glasses again. Nigel touched
her shoulder and said, 'You'll be able to make out the villa
in a few minutes. You'll get a shower and a rest then. It's
been a tiring trip, hasn't it?'

She wasn't tired, but it was very hot, even the moving
air on their faces was hot, and a shower would be lovely.
Although she would rather have slipped down for a swim
in the deep green water. She suggested, 'How about swimming for it?' joking, and he said quite seriously,

'The swimming's good, but this isn't a swimming pool.'

'I can see that,' she said, and thought, You don't even
know that I'm a strong swimmer. You think my limit is a
few lengths in a pool.

'I can see Jotham!' squealed Erica, with a pair of binoculars to her eyes. 'He's waiting for us on the jetty.' The
binoculars were handed round: Annie next, then Harriet.

'Where's the villa?' asked Harriet.

'Just up from the beach,' said Nigel. 'Get the sea line
and straight ahead. Joth's on the jetty.'

She would see him soon enough. She found the villa,
a long low white building with yellow shutters and red-
pantiled roof. She could make out a verandah, and splashes
of colour that were plants in pots. Then she scanned down-
wards toward the beach and once the figures came into
view she had to look at them.

There was another man with him, someone shorter, thinner, dark. They were both wearing shirts that looked ragged from here, and they were talking, laughing. It seemed odd not to hear the laughter when she could see Jotham laughing so clearly.

'Finished?' asked Erica, and Harriet was taking longer than her share. She handed back the glasses.

'Sorry,' she said, 'but I haven't see the place before. The villa looks interesting.'

They all assured her that it was and she asked, 'Who's the other man on the jetty?'

'I thought you were looking at the villa,' said Erica.

I do wish you were Annie, thought Harriet. I'd have no scruples in giving you an unfair fight, but I hate the thought of hurting Annie. 'And like I said,' said Harriet, 'the villa looks interesting. Who's the other man?'

Nigel told her he was Paolo, that his parents Angelo and Elena were housekeeper and gardener at the villa, and soon she could see the men on the jetty without needing binoculars.

She could see the villa too, of course, and the oranges and lemons on the trees, but her eyes kept flickering back to the jetty and Jotham Gaul. The easy relaxing time was over. A feeling like prickly heat was running up and down her spine and irritating her skin. That was her nerves playing up at the sight of him. She scratched her arm, and looked at the reddening of the skin on the golden tan, and thought—he's bringing me up in heat bumps, I am definitely allergic to him.

The fishing boat had been moored alongside the jetty, fastened by Jotham to a bollard. As soon as it was fairly steady everybody started jumping out and tossing out luggage. Everybody, including the two fishermen who had ferried them over, seemed to be talking and laughing. Joth was doing the welcoming. Both Annie and Erica had run into his arms, and he kissed them both, and somehow still kept his arms around them while he was shaking hands with Alistair and clapping Nigel on the shoulder.

Paolo was grinning at everybody. He was older than Harriet had expected him to be, with a very dark, very wrinkled face and black close-cut curly hair. He gave Harriet a smiling nod. Nigel had helped her on to the quayside and now she stood there, apart from all this mutual admiration.

She was wearing a plain white dress that showed off the tan of her smooth arms and legs, white flat-thonged sandals and a white scarf tying back her hair. She was looking cooler than she felt. She felt as if her clothes were sticking to her, plastered to her slippery skin. Jotham looked bigger than ever and more rugged. That shirt *was* torn, and open to the waist. His sandals were covered with dust and there was a daub of what looked like grey paint down the side of his trousers. He looked like a beachcomber down on his luck, except that everyone was milling around him, as though he was king.

Over their heads his eyes met Harriet's. 'Good lord!' he exclaimed. 'You!' And she thought incredulously, I do believe he forgot I was coming. But of course he hadn't. He was just telling everybody how unimportant and easy to forget she was.

'Immaculate as ever,' he added, and she flashed a false smile, simpering in a wicked take-off of a Southern belle.

'Aren't you the flatterer, and me in this old thing?' She looked up at the big house. 'And what a darling little place you have here!'

'It has been,' he said, and he grinned coming towards her, leaving Erica and Annie and the rest and the cases strewn around. Harriet stood with folded arms, annoyed with herself because she badly wanted to sidestep, to get round him to the others. But she didn't. She stood still, and looked at him through her dark glasses, which were large and round enough to mask the upper part of her face, as she waited for what he had come over here to say. Whatever it was she didn't care. He couldn't do a thing to her, unless he fancied his chances of crowding her off the jetty.

When he was close enough to touch her she found she was holding her breath, rigid and hostile, then he leaned over smiling and took off her glasses. She had never thought he would dare to touch her, except perhaps to take her arm or hand, mocking as she had, pretending to welcome her.

When his fingers brushed her cheeks and her hair she jerked her head back and her eyes flew open as though he had touched a wild nerve. It hurt, the sudden light blazing on her, the man looking straight into her eyes. 'Ah yes,' he drawled, 'it's you all right,' and he replaced her glasses so that the whipping off and the replacement seemed like one smooth movement.

But behind them Harriet shut her eyes tightly for a moment. He knows I'm afraid of him, she thought, and she felt cold in the fierce heat of the day, because until then she hadn't known it herself.

They were picking up the cases, and there was a box of provisions that had been brought over in the fishing boat. Everything had to be carried along the jetty and across the beach and then up steps cut in the rock. Harriet took it for granted that the men would do the carrying. She took a few steps swinging her handbag and Jotham called, 'Don't go empty-handed.'

She knew he was speaking to her, and she turned unwillingly and took the small case he was holding out. 'I don't know whether it was mentioned to you,' he said, 'but nobody gets waited on here.'

'That's all right by me,' she drawled, and it was easy

along the jetty, harder across the strip of beach, and a real haul climbing the rough uneven steps hacked in the rocks. The heat would have made the lightest load heavy, and it didn't improve Harriet's temper to see that Erica was climbing empty-handed, Joth hadn't called her back.

Nigel, with a case in either hand, stayed just behind Harriet warning her, 'Mind this step, it's cracked,' or 'Careful now!' Harriet turned to look back at him once and saw Annie's woebegone face and knew that the last time they were here Nigel was probably telling Annie to watch how she went.

Then Jotham said something very quietly that made Annie laugh, and Harriet was sure it was a crack at her expense.

Where the rock steps ended a wooden staircase led up to the verandah. There had been recent repairs done to this, the new wood was conspicuous, and now you could see how badly the whole place needed repainting. The white house, the yellow shutters, had faded and peeled; but the big stone and terra-cotta pots on the verandah were full of brightly coloured flowers and plants. At the corners of the verandah were almost life-size statues in flowing classical draperies. Dark with age, they looked as though the Romans just might have left them behind. A small garrison had been stationed here, briefly, two thousand years ago.

The shutters and the central door were closed and Harriet hurried to get inside, not only because it would be cooler there but because she wanted to see.

She wasn't disappointed. She stepped into a huge entrance-hall-cum-drawing-room, the light filtering in thin patterns through the frescoed shutters on to a floor tiled in marble slabs the colour of deep blue-green water. Chairs were covered in faded threadbare brocade in greens and blues, and it was cool and she loved it.

If it had belonged to anyone else she would have bubbled over with enthusiasm, because this had been a beautiful house. Pictures had gone from the walls, the plaster was faded and cracked, but the furniture was good—what there was of it. There were closed doors on either side and a wide heavily carved staircase in the centre.

On top of the carved posts were two sitting beasts, lions probably, holding shields with almost identical coats of arms. Harriet walked across to examine them and looked up at Joth. 'Not your coat of arms, I suppose?' she said.

He grinned. 'There'd be a bar sinister across it if it was. I'm a bastard,' and she couldn't help her lips twitching as she retorted,

'You can say that again!'

It had taken a moment or two to get used to the shadowy light in here. She had put her case down, looked around and walked over to the staircase, but now she saw the man and woman, darkly clad, who were talking in English to Nigel and the others. The newcomers were saying how glad they were to be here again, the woman was saying how glad she and her husband were to see them once more.

'Angelo and Elena?' asked Harriet softly.

'Yes,' said Joth.

The woman was very upright, dressed from head to foot in black, and wearing a black headscarf and large gold hoop earrings. Harriet guessed that she was around seventy years of age. The man stooped like a gnarled old tree, but both seemed alert and both were smiling.

'Does Paolo work here too?' Harriet asked.

'He's a goatherd. They're the entire staff at present,' said Joth.

She could see why, in a place this size, visitors were expected to care for themselves, and she followed Joth to be introduced. Elena was a dignified old lady but her eyes, on Harriet, were gleaming with curiosity. Harriet was the odd-girl-out. These friends of Signor Gaul's were husband and wife, and almost-affianced, so where did this girl with the so-beautiful hair belong? Another special friend of the Signore's, perhaps?

Their rooms were ready, Elena informed them all. The same rooms. Harriet caught Annie's look of dismay and Joth said, 'We'll take the cases up.' There were ten bedrooms, Harriet remembered hearing, so even if Nigel and Annie had shared a room before there was no reason they shouldn't sleep apart now. She was sure that Joth would not let Annie be embarrassed. Another room would soon be found for Annie.

Angelo picked up Harriet's cases and Elena led the way to her room, along a passage that went straight ahead from the top of the stairs, with doors regularly placed along it. Harriet's room was at the end of the passage where Angelo put down the cases and left, while Elena waited to hear if there was anything else that the latest guest required.

A large blue pitcher filled with water stood in a matching bowl. A shower could come later, this would do for now, and Harriet said, 'Thank you. It all looks lovely.' The furniture was elegant: wardrobe, bedhead, dressing table and bureau in inlaid walnut; and Elena smiled, accepting the compliment, and Harriet added casually, 'Which is Mr Gaul's room?'

Elena's smile became rather knowing; she inclined her head towards the wall, presumably meaning next door.

'You are so wrong,' Harriet could have said. 'Although I didn't expect him to be far away.' She went to the window and raised the blind, and heard the rustle of skirts as the housekeeper left the room.

There was a balcony out there, but she would have preferred a window facing the sea. This was an awesome view, with the dark grey volcano dominating the skyline.

She opened the window and sniffed, wrinkling her nose, trying to separate the scents: sharp citrus, a musky smell that might be the olive trees, a faint undernote of sulphur. Everything was still, without a breath of air; and quiet, with no sign of a single bird. Whether the volcano was extinct or not—and it was, the men who knew about that sort of thing were all agreed—this volcanic island had a feeling of something primitive and powerful, that might one day wake terribly from sleep.

If it does, Harriet thought, I hope I get fair warning. I can well imagine Jotham forgetting to load me on the boat.

She unpacked, and washed from head to foot in the soft lukewarm water. Then she covered herself in suntan oil before putting on a bikini under a white cotton blouse and a blue skirt. By the end of her holiday she would have a terrific tan as her skin soaked up the sun. She had been pale lately, but she was looking browner and healthier every day.

She was the last one down. Nigel was waiting for her in the hall and the rest were sitting around the kitchen table. She heard their voices through the open door as she came down the stairs, and saw Nigel standing alone at the foot of the staircase, and quickened her step. She apologised, 'I'm afraid I took my time.'

'You look wonderful,' he said ardently. 'Gleaming like a golden goddess.'

'A bit sticky,' she shrugged. 'The gleam's suntan oil. Do I smell food?'

The soup was a fish soup with semolina pasta, followed by little fried pastries containing cheese and sugar, great bowls of fruit, goat butter with rough nutty bread, and sweetish local red and white wine.

In the old days Elena had been first on the cooking staff in the villa and for many years the housekeeper. Angelo had always worked in the gardens, and during the decline in the fortunes of the Raffaeles both had stayed on, while one by one the rest of the staff died or left the island.

This was their home. Where else could they go? There was no room in their son Paolo's little house, and after the Contessa died, and the villa stood empty for nearly two years, they carried on with their tasks. Without pay, there hadn't been much in the way of wages for a long time. Neither spoke of the dread of a new owner who might turn them out, not even to each other, and then Jotham Gaul came, greeting them with courtesy, listening to them, rather than to the sharp man with the city ways who was representing the last of the Raffaeles who had never set foot on the island.

There was talk of other houses being built, but when Jotham Gaul smiled Elena knew that the villa was safe and so were they. 'The Blessed Virgin be praised,' she said to Angelo. 'He is a good man,' and Elena was a fine judge of character; Angelo had never known her wrong.

Visitors had come to the villa since then, and both Elena and Angelo enjoyed that. It kept the house alive, and they treated Elena and Angelo with respect, as the Signore did. At first Elena had been shocked at the idea of letting them work, preparing meals, keeping bedrooms in order, washing, cleaning. She and Angelo were receiving a salary again. But perhaps she could not have coped single-handed and they made a game of it. Some day there would be other paid staff and she would be in charge, the housekeeper. The Signore had told her that.

Erica and Annie were discussing menus—working out a list of provisions to be delivered by one of the fishing boats from the mainland—when Harriet sat down at the table. She ate her soup in silence until Erica asked, 'Are you a good cook?'

'No,' said Harriet. 'But I'm sure you are.'

'Cordon Bleu,' said Alistair, and Erica looked smug.

'And Annie has cooked some of the best meals I've ever eaten,' said Jotham, which made Annie smile. Harriet appreciated that Annie needed somebody to speak up for her, but it would be a bore if this went on, Jotham seizing every opportunity to praise Annie and make Harriet look inferior.

'And you've eaten a few good meals in your time, haven't you?' she said sourly. 'You're reaching the age when you should start watching that waistline.'

Both Erica and Annie broke out in protests, although Jotham only grinned, and Harriet said, 'Well, don't sign me on as cook, because I can't boil an egg.'

That wasn't true. She could manage around a stove if she had to, but she had never done much cooking and she was certainly not putting down full platters for Jotham Gaul.

'What can you do?' he asked her, and Nigel said fatuously,

'Look beautiful. A girl who looks like Harriet doesn't have to do anything else.'

Silence fell. You tactless idiot, Harriet thought wearily. She could see Erica hating her, Annie's smile frozen on her lips. And it was no compliment, being told she was nothing but an ornament. She said quickly, 'It's make-up, most of it. Tricks of the modelling trade.'

The only make-up she was wearing was oil, but Annie and Erica began to look intrigued, and Harriet went on, 'If we don't need another cook how about a cleaner? I'll do the washing up or make the beds. Just tell me what. Of course I'll earn my keep.'

'Of course you will,' said Jotham cheerfully. 'There's never been any question about that.'

When the meal was over they went down to the beach and lazed, sunbathing on the silvery sand. The water looked cool under the burning blue sky, and Harriet had just

decided it must be safe by now to go swimming when Erica
got up. 'Coming in?' she said to everybody, and to Harriet,
'I suppose you can swim?'

'Yes,' said Harriet.

'See that rock?' There were several rocks in the little
bay, Erica was pointing at the biggest, a flat-topped rock
about fifty yards out. 'Can you reach that?'

'I should think so,' said Harriet.

'Race you!' said Erica, and ran splashing into the water,
followed by Annie and Alistair. Nigel held out a hand to
Harriet, and she went with him into the gently lapping
waves, realising after they had swum a few strokes side
by side that she could outstrip Nigel and probably the
rest of them.

She was a strong swimmer, but winning this race wasn't
going to endear her to anybody. Why not let Erica get to
the rock first? Or Alistair. He was forging on nicely with
his crawl, and Annie was doing a brisk breast stroke.

'Thank you for bringing me here,' she said.

They reached the rock and clambered up, the girls shaking their wet hair out of their eyes. Jotham was still on
the beach, he hadn't accepted the challenge and Harriet
thought—if he had I wouldn't have been able to help myself going all out. I couldn't have let him get ahead of me
without a fight.

Perhaps he wasn't much of a swimmer. Perhaps she could
wait until he got out of his depth and grab his ankles and
pull him under. It would be very satisfying to see him
bob up again puffing and blowing.

She asked, 'Isn't Jotham joining us?'

Everybody said he would be and they larked about,
diving and jumping off the rock, churning up the water
around it.

On one side of the little bay, beyond the jetty, a project-
ing flat rock jutted out. The water would always be deep

there and it would make a splendid diving board at high
tide. She must ask about submerged rocks sometime, but
not right now because Nigel was making a fuss of taking
care of her, as though she was only a fair-to-average swimmer.

'I'm all right,' she told him at last, getting tired of it.
'Stop fussing!' Then she felt guilty and smiled to take the
sting from the snub. 'I'm good at floating,' she said. 'When
I'm tired of sitting here I'll float for a bit.'

She stayed on the big flat-topped rock when the rest
set off for other rocks. The sun was still dazzling, making
the water look like shifting silver, and as soon as she was
alone she slipped into the sea, and kicked away on her
back, sculling herself smoothly.

She could almost have fallen asleep, it was like lying
on a waterbed being rocked gently, lovingly. After a while
she heard her name called and raised an arm and waved
and called back 'Hello!' She rather hoped Nigel wouldn't
join her. She was enjoying being alone. She didn't want
to talk or play tag, just go on floating, lifting her head occasionally to look at the coastline and the gnarled trees of
the fruit groves, and the villa and the volcano.

Nigel didn't come, and after a few more minutes she
let her legs drop and trod water, upright, the water lapping
over her shoulders, and looked around for him. He was
sitting on the big rock, talking to Jotham, and Harriet was
convinced they were discussing her.

She couldn't hear them, but there were only the two of
them in what seemed to be a serious conversation. The
others were bobbing around farther out, she counted heads,
and she felt the gentle tug of a current and went with it
a little way. Whatever Jotham was saying to Nigel she
wanted to break it up, and that meant either swimming
back or getting Nigel over here—and she grinned, suddenly, mischievously.

She could let Nigel save her. She could call for help and
have him steaming to the rescue. Cramp maybe, although
the water was rather warm for cramp. The current then,
pulling her, making her realise that she was tired.

She flung up both arms and screeched, 'Nigel, help
me! There's a current, it's pulling ...' Then she took a
lungful of air and ducked under, swimming down deep and
staying down for about twenty-five seconds. As she started
to float up again, somebody seized her, indistinct through
the bubbling turbulence, taking her up. When they broke
through to the surface she saw it was Joth and spat. 'You!'

'Drowners can't be choosers,' he said. He went over on
his back, never losing hold of her, and she guessed that if
she had fought he would have dealt with her resistance
none too gently. He knew she wasn't drowning, and he set
off back to the beach taking her along, holding her under
the water as often as over.

Of course it was deliberate. He wanted her choking and
spluttering, looking a fool, and admitting she had been
fooling Nigel. He was trying to scare her, so she gulped in
breath when she could and wasted no strength in strug-
gling.

When he stopped swimming and stood she went limp.
She might just scare him a little, he might not be quite
so sure this time that she wasn't in genuine distress. At
least this way she'd get Nigel's sympathy.

She kept her eyes closed and felt herself being carried
a short distance and then dropped on the beach. She felt
Jotham beside her and she heard him say softly in her
ear, 'I advise you to come round very quickly indeed unless
you want me to give you the kiss of life.'

She opened her eyes then. He was leaning over her so
that water dripped from his face on to hers. 'Get off me!'
she spluttered.

'I'm not on you,' he pointed out, 'not yet.' That was

the literal truth, but she felt as though he was pressing her down into the sand, which was hot and gritty under her wet skin. 'How about this kiss of life?' he said, and she shot up so suddenly that their foreheads bumped and she winced and muttered.

'You're like hitting a rock. You'd be a real hazard submerged out there.'

Then Nigel was calling her name, and everybody was coming in out of the sea. Nigel reached her first, flinging himself down on his knees beside her, asking, 'Are you all right?'

'I think so,' she said.

The others were less impressed, although Alistair looked quite concerned. Annie was biting her lip thoughtfully and Erica drawled, 'What happened then? I thought you could swim.'

Harriet reached to brush sand from her shoulders, where it was sticking and itching, and Nigel went to collect one of the towels they had brought down to the beach. She had swallowed so much sea water that she was beginning to feel queasy.

'Better stay in your depth next time,' said Joth, and they all knew from his grin that she had been pretending panic and the laugh was on her. Nigel came with a large towel and wrapped it around her and she said,

'I think I'll go in. I feel as if I've swallowed half the bay.'

'You don't look as elegant as usual,' said Joth, and she said,

'I've had a narrow escape. It could have been very nasty.'

'Come off it,' said Erica scornfully. 'You were in no danger. Any of us could have got you out.'

'Who's talking about drowning?' said Harriet. 'Of course I wasn't drowning. I was fooling about.' Everybody knew that, so she might as well admit it. She grimaced, pucker-

ing her mouth. 'But I nearly got the kiss of life from
Joth,' she added, 'and I can't think of many things more
likely to finish me than that.'

They all laughed then, including Joth. Whether it was
with her or at her she didn't know. Nor did she much care.
'I'm going in,' she said again, and she went with the towel
wrapped around her across to the pile of sandals, selecting
her own, and set off across the stony shingle to the foot
of the steps cut in the rock.

Nigel was just behind her. 'Dinner's about seven,' he
said.

'Uh-huh.'

'You are all right?'

She said huffily, 'I was better before he got hold of me.
He nearly did darn well drown me!'

'I'm sorry about that,' said Nigel, 'but you really sounded
as though you were in trouble. Joth's a better swimmer
than I am. He got to you first. When he found you weren't,
well——'

Harriet said tartly, 'I'm surprised he bothered. If he
thought I was in trouble I'd have thought he'd have let me
sink.'

They were at the top of the rock steps, and she paused
before walking up the shorter wooden flight to the verandah. The others were still on the beach. Their voices and
their laughter rose on the breathless air. 'Which is your
room?' Nigel asked her.

'The one next to Joth's.' She climbed the wooden steps
and sat down on one of the little white-painted cane chairs
on the verandah. It had been quite a climb, after being
dragged underwater across the bay, and she needed a rest.
She could still see the beach from here, and the others.
The girls were at the water's edge again. The men were
sitting together talking. She wondered if that was about

the holiday development. It would make a lot of money, she supposed, but she was glad she had come to the island while everything was unchanged and unspoiled.

Nigel had been telling her that he and Annie had been put in the same room, but now he was at the top of the stairs in a room of his own and she had nodded, thinking of other things. 'And you're next to Joth?' said Nigel.

She nodded again. 'Like it was in your house.' Nigel had seated himself in a chair beside her. In front of them was a round cane matching table, and this would be a good place to drink long cold drinks. But perhaps a shower and a rest would be more refreshing. Harriet said, 'Your mother put me there so that Joth could warn me off you and keep an eye on me, I suppose. She's very pro-Annie, of course, and so's he, isn't he?'

'They get on very well.'

'If he's so struck with her why doesn't *he* marry her?'

Nigel laughed at that. 'Joth isn't the marrying type. Girls go for him, but I can't ever see him settling down with one.' He grinned. 'I think my mother hoped you might go for Joth too.'

'What?' Harriet screeched. 'I thought she was fond of him. I thought he was like another son to her. If she thinks I'd be so bad for you why should she think I'd be all right for him?'

Nigel went on smiling, with the note of envy in his voice that she had heard before. 'Joth can handle glamorous ladies, and afford them. He never really gets involved. Everybody has a good time and they go on being good friends.'

'Well, I've had enough of his handling, thank you!' Harriet slid the towel off her shoulders and looked for bruises. 'And somebody should tell your mother that there is no way Jotham Gaul and I are going to end up good friends.'

Much less lovers on the way. That thought made her skin crawl. She felt it quicken, all her nerves protesting, and Nigel said huskily, 'Your eyes are such a fantastic green.'

She need never be afraid when Nigel looked into her eyes. All he would see was their colour and the thick spiky fringe of lashes. It was Jotham who looked deep and whose gaze she was afraid to meet.

She stood up and picked up the towel, and said, 'Please show me where the showers are.'

Nigel bent his head to kiss her bare shoulder. 'Afterwards——?' he said, and she said briskly,

'Afterwards I'm resting for a while. And I do mean resting.'

The shower room led off a downstairs bathroom and she showered quickly, washing her hair, and met no one as she walked through the entrance hall and up the staircase to her bedroom. She couldn't hear voices either, so she presumed the others were still down on the beach.

In her room she locked her door, then sat on the bed brushing and drying her hair with her little battery-operated dryer. 'You don't look as elegant as usual,' Jotham had said when he'd landed her on the sand like something the tide had washed up. But she would go down to dinner tonight looking as glamorous as any of his ladies.

How many had he had, for goodness' sake? Not that she was competing. If she was doing this for anybody but herself she was doing it for Nigel. She had put down the hairdryer for a moment when the knock came on the door and she froze. Soon there was a second tap and Nigel called 'Harriet, it's me.' He was speaking very close to the door panel and very quietly, and she could have opened the door and said, 'Please go away, I need my siesta.' But she had told him she was going to rest, and if she did nothing at all he would think she was asleep. That wouldn't hurt his feelings. That wasn't a rejection.

She didn't consider letting him in, although she was here because she was hoping to fall in love with him. She found him attractive, he was a very attractive man, knocking on her door, wanting her. But she sat, still as a mouse, not making a sound, waiting for him to go away.

CHAPTER SIX

HARRIET stayed in her room until it was almost time for dinner, and then she made an entrance down the staircase. The entrance wasn't planned for effect, although she had dressed to catch the eye as she usually did. She was wearing a long white silk tunic, clipped at the shoulders, clinched at the waist, split at the sides, half a dozen thin gold chains, and flat golden sandals.

The others were down already, and when Harriet appeared at the top of the stairs they all turned to look at her. She could stand their scrutiny, she was used to being stared at, and she continued to walk calmly down the centre of the wide staircase while Joth gave her an ironic round of applause.

'What an entrance,' he grinned as she reached the bottom step, and she grinned back,

'I'm glad you enjoyed it. I do find that the setting helps tremendously. I couldn't have done it without your staircase.'

'Feel free to come down any time,' he told her, and Nigel said solemnly,

'You look more like a goddess than ever tonight.' There was something Grecian or Roman about the softly flowing tunic, but the compliment embarrassed her. Annie couldn't enjoy hearing him continually raving about Harriet's looks.

'Or a slave girl,' said Jotham, and she was glad to get back to flippancy, retorting,

'Don't bank on that when you're allocating the chores

tomorrow. And talking of chores, who cooked tonight's dinner?'

On this first night it was Elena, with no help from anyone, and a very good meal it was. They ate on the verandah, two little round tables drawn together, while the stars came out in the sky and the moon rode high; and across the bay the fishing fleet passed, lights bobbing on bows and sterns like dancing stars in the water.

Harriet sat quietly. She didn't want to spoil the peaceful feeling, so she ate her meal and drank her wine and listened while they talked about the *festa*, dedicated to a local saint, but held the day after tomorrow in the ruins of a tiny Roman temple on the slopes of the volcano. The fishermen from the mainland brought over families and sweethearts and food and drink, and the islanders laid on a local spread. There was music and dancing and a contest to find which man could throw the discus farthest and Jotham—the only one who had been here for the last year's *festa*—said that it had been a rattling good party.

Harriet thought it sounded a happy occasion, and she was intrigued by the Roman remains. She must find out where they were. There was a lot of exploring she wanted to do. She was determined to enjoy this holiday in spite of Jotham Gaul.

'Shall we go inside?' said Jotham when the meal was over, and a door was open in the hall showing a glimpse of a well lighted room. There was still the villa to explore as well as the island, but for Harriet it could all wait till tomorrow, and Annie was yawning and Erica said, 'I guess I'll say goodnight.'

The men were staying down a little longer, and the three girls went upstairs. Erica's room came first. She went in without a word and Annie called, 'Goodnight,' as the door shut.

'Goodnight,' said Harriet to the closed door, and Annie gave her a faint smile.

'I was jealous of her,' said Annie, 'the last time we came here, in the spring, because she's so much better looking than I am. And now there's you, and Erica's jealous. I don't suppose you've ever envied anybody in your life, have you?'

'Quite a few,' said Harriet. Looks weren't all you needed for happiness by a long chalk. She asked impulsively, 'Are you very fond of Nigel?' and could have bitten her tongue because it was the last thing she wanted to know.

'Yes,' said Annie. She had stopped at what was obviously her door. 'I thought we'd be getting engaged at the *festa*. Are you fond of him?'

'Yes,' said Harriet.

'Well, he's daft about you,' said Annie with a spurt of unexpected spirit. 'And I don't know what I'm doing here. I wouldn't have come if Jotham hadn't said I ought to. I hadn't seen you then, of course. If I had seen you I wouldn't have bothered.'

She marched into her room and shut the door, and Harriet sighed. So Annie was here at Joth's personal urging, and what was that about getting engaged at the *festa*? Nobody had mentioned that before.

What with Annie and Erica and Joth all against her there might not be much opportunity for long walks and quiet talks with Nigel. Instead of getting to know him, and her own feelings for him, in a civilised atmosphere, there was more likelihood of rows and slanging matches. Erica had been sniping at her ever since they'd met and Annie had just gone off like a crackerjack.

That was bad enough, but if Joth ever blew his top it would be the real thing, like the volcano going up, and she wondered if getting to know Nigel would be worth the stress and strain. Oh, she was fond enough of him, and if he was serious about her then he would do the seeking out. But right now she didn't feel like taking the initiative.

It was still hot. Even after Harriet had stripped and washed she still felt sticky. She couldn't bear even a sheet on her skin and she lay on top of the bed, thinking of the sea just out there, moon silver now, cooler than the bright white glitter of the sun.

She imagined herself floating again, the slow lift and fall of the water, and as that soothed her nearer sleep she remembered Jotham catching her under the waves, taking her to the surface. He would have saved her if she had been in danger. He had been the one to reach her when she called for help. He might be Annie's champion, but he had answered Harriet's cry.

She tossed again for a few seconds and thought—the first thing that's needed here is an air-conditioning system if the generator could run to it, then she slipped into unconsciousness ...

She woke as though someone had jerked her from sleep, startled and alert, and sat up looking around the darkened room. There was a feeling of movement, a faint trembling like an underground train in the far distance, just for a moment.

An earth tremor? The *volcano*? Who said it was dead? Who really knew? Was there even a boat on the island if they had to get away?

She was out of bed, grabbing a green silk kimono and pulling it on, tying the sash. Then she opened the long window and stepped on to the balcony looking up at the looming shape, half expecting to see a glow around the rim. There were thin clouds floating in the sky up there, or maybe wisps of smoke.

No lights shone from the house, so it must be late, and was it possible that nobody else had felt the tremor? Everything was steady now, except for a breeze rustling the leaves of the trees. But she hadn't dreamt it. It had woken her and she had been awake and felt it, and she had to tell somebody, and hear what they had to tell her, before she could contemplate going back to bed and trying to sleep again.

The window of the room she supposed was Joth's was a little way open and she peered in, making out a shape in the bed. 'I say,' she said, then raised her voice and said, 'Excuse me.'

He sat up. It was Joth, and she coughed, clearing her throat that had practically closed from fear. 'It's Harriet,' she croaked.

'I can see it's Harriet.' She was revealingly outlined and she clutched her kimono tighter around her. 'Sorry, Harriet,' he drawled, 'you've got the wrong room.'

'Didn't you feel that shaking just now?' Her voice was quivering. 'My bed shook. Are you sure this thing is harmless?'

'Oh, that wasn't ours. That was a murmur from one of the others on the mainland. Vibrations travel, it's nothing to worry about. Ours went up for the last time while the Roman outpost was here.'

He was so calm that she believed him, although she demanded, 'You're sure we're not about due again?'

'We're extinct,' he said. 'I'm sorry you were scared.'

Are you heck! she thought. You wouldn't have cared if I'd had screaming hysterics. She said coolly, 'I'm sorry I disturbed you, but nobody told me to expect the shakes,' and she turned to look up at the volcano again. It looked cold now, a great grey mountain, and the clouds were clouds and not in the least like smoke. She took two steps to the balcony's edge and stood clutching the little rail of the balustrade. Everything felt steady as a rock, and she heard Joth step out and then he was standing beside her, barefoot, wearing a camel dressing gown.

'And I haven't seen a boat moored around here,' she said, 'and I wasn't sure you'd let me aboard if we did have to evacuate.'

'Now why should you think you'd be abandoned after the way I've already saved you from drowning?'

'The way you nearly did drown me, you mean.' Then she smiled with a sidewards glance at him. 'Did you know I was fooling until you reached me?'

'No, although if I'd stopped to think I'd have known.' It was a bright night, almost as clear as a dark day. She could see him plainly, and not just the bulk of him, but the expression, the ruffled hair. She held on to the balcony rail and he stood, hands in pockets, watching her. 'That's one of your ploys, isn't it?' he said. 'The weak little woman. Fainting. Drowning.'

'No, it is not,' she snapped. 'Do I look like a weak little woman?' and he chuckled.

'I didn't say you were one. I said you played the part when it suited you.'

Harriet didn't have to defend herself to him, but she said, 'I was fooling in the water, but I did faint back at Tudor House. It was the first time I've ever fainted, but it was the first time I ever stopped eating and I never lost my father before.'

He said, 'I'm sorry,' and she said quietly,

'I loved him, you know.'

Now why had she said that? She didn't want his sympathy.

'Is that why you turned to Nigel? Is it some sort of security you're looking for?' he asked her, and she didn't want him probing her motives either.

'I told you I wanted to live in Tudor House,' she said, and that came uncomfortably close to the truth. Her feelings for Nigel were bound up with that house, and the New Year's Eve party when it was all beginning and her father was proud of her for the first time.

'Why don't you mind your own business?' she snapped. 'How do you know Nigel and I aren't right for each other?'

He looked at her for what seemed a long time, then he said, 'Poor Annie doesn't have much chance,' and although that might have been a compliment it only made her angry.

'You are so sorry for her, aren't you?' she said, and he agreed.

'Of course I'm sorry for her. She's a grand girl, and the man everyone expected her to marry, and she expected to marry, is sleeping with——'

'Not with me he isn't!' Harriet got that in fierce and fast as though he had to be told, although again it was none of his business.

'Not tonight,' he corrected.

'Not any night. So far.'

There was another silence, then he said, 'Why not? I thought he was supposed to be finding you irresistible.'

She shrugged. Lack of opportunity up to a point, but she could have been with Nigel tonight. She could have run for Nigel when she felt that earth tremor, and she wondered why she hadn't, instead of sticking her head through Jotham Gaul's window.

She said lightly, 'Perhaps I'm resisting for a while. And Nigel has good manners, he waits to be asked. Nigel would never kick down a lady's door.'

'Don't look at me,' said Jotham in mock indignation. 'I don't go around kicking in doors. I don't need to, they come in through the window,' and Harriet gurgled,

'And then find they're in the wrong room?'

'You can't win them all.'

'I've been hearing that you win most of them.'

'I have heard that you do.'

This was the teasing talk of friends, and a sudden light breeze flapped the silken skirt around her bare legs, and she thought—what am I doing out here, practically naked, chatting up Jotham Gaul?

She turned towards her window. 'Goodnight, then,' she said, 'and please keep our volcano quiet.'

'I'll do that for you.' Something in the timbre of his voice made her hesitate, and look back as though he hadn't finished talking. But he didn't say any more, and she went into her room and closed the long window. She shut it tight, then crossed to the bed and lay down, still wearing her silk kimono.

She couldn't have been outside longer than a couple of minutes. Fear, anger, laughing together, in such a brief time. What might have been next? Suppose Jotham had drawn her close when she was afraid? She would have been astounded of course, and furious. But just now, while they were laughing, if he had reached for her hand she might have gone on smiling.

I would not, she decided, and neither would he; he's always disliked me and he always will. But she fell asleep still puzzling over the way he had sounded, almost as though he didn't want her to go in. If she hadn't said goodnight how long would they have stayed talking to each other? she wondered. What else might have been said? Or done...?

She thought about it again when she woke up. She lay for five minutes or so going over those few minutes on the balcony, and decided that nothing had changed. Jotham Gaul wouldn't be on her side if the end of the world came and only the two of them were left, but he was a surprising man.

She got up, dressed, and went downstairs. It was early, the heat of the day would come later. Now might be the time to go exploring, if somebody would tell her where the Roman ruins were. Or to climb to the summit of the volcano and look in, and reassure herself finally that nothing was bubbling down there.

She met nobody until she walked into the kitchen where Angelo and Annie were sitting at the table drinking coffee, eating hot croissants and preserves; and Elena was chopping red and green peppers, with a deadly-looking knife on a chopping board.

'Good morning,' said Harriet, and Angelo and Elena said, '*Buon giorno, signorina,*' and Annie said, 'Help yourself,' pointing at the coffee pot.

Harriet poured herself a cup and asked, 'Are we the only ones down?'

'Jotham's around,' said Annie. Of course Annie would know that, Harriet reflected, as she drank her coffee, while Annie and Elena went on discussing *festa* food.

The Villa Raffaele had always provided the feast in the old days, but less and less during the lean years. Now the Villa had a Signore again and last year, given a free hand by Jotham Gaul, Elena had done everybody proud. She was looking forward to putting on an even better spread this year.

'More coffee?' Annie offered Harriet. 'And perhaps another cup for Joth.'

She poured into a clean cup first and Harriet surprised herself by saying, 'Shall I take it to him?'

'If you like.' Annie sounded surprised too. 'He's in the office. Through the *salotto*, that's the first door across the hall.'

So here was Harriet carrying a cup of coffee for the master. Nobody could say she wasn't being helpful. The *salotto* was the door that had been open last night and something of a surprise because it had been recently decorated. The contrast between the peeling walls of the entrance hall and these walls, unmarked matt dark blue under a cool grey ceiling, was striking. There were Persian rugs on this floor and the furniture had a Regency style.

A portrait of a young woman immediately caught the

eye, painted in what might have been this room. There was
a window in the background and through it a grove of
lemon trees. She looked haughty and handsome, shining
black hair in a chignon, pearls round her throat and rings
on her fingers, and as she passed the painting Harriet said,
'Who might you be, I wonder?'

The door at the far end had to lead to the office, so she
tapped on it and Jotham called, 'Come in.'

His eyebrows rose when he saw her. He was behind a
big desk and two piles of papers, one on his left and one
on his right. Between them he had a typescript and he
seemed to be writing comments in the margin.

Harriet couldn't help seeing all this because she was
looking for a space to put down the coffee cup. She said,
'Annie sent you this.'

'Annie's a thoughtful girl.' Joth reached across the desk
and took the cup from her.

'Aren't you on holiday?' she asked.

'Another half hour and I am.' The piles of papers fascinated her for some reason. She stood there looking at
them, until he said, 'Anything else?'

The island seemed so far removed from the world of
business. She went on looking at the papers. 'Is there a
mail service?'

'The fishing boats bring in the mail bags. Do you want to
send some letters?'

Harriet shook her head. 'Not particularly. It just seems
odd to see you still running your empire from here. Are any
of these anything to do with my factory?' She changed that
before he could. 'My factory that's practically yours.'

'Yes,' he said, and of course that was why she couldn't
take her eyes off the papers. It wasn't her factory any more,
but she was still interested, still concerned.

'Will you make it pay?' she asked.

'Yes.'

'How?'

'New machinery. New markets.' He was reading while he was speaking, his attention on the figures and the type-written words, and it sounded as simple as a magician saying, 'Abracadabra'.

When she had first met him Nigel had said something about a factory up north.

Harriet heard herself ask, 'How did you start? Where did you come from?' and without raising his eyes Joth said,

'All you need worry about is that I'm here now.'

'Saving Nigel for Annie.' She wanted to make him look up, but he didn't.

'Among other things,' he said, and she jeered,

'You run half a dozen factories before breakfast, which leaves you the rest of the day for running other people's lives, and that's your idea of a holiday?' Then he looked up.

'Go and amuse yourself somewhere else,' he said, and Harriet banged the door childishly as she went out. She hadn't really expected Jotham would discuss his plans for the factory with her. Or that he would start telling her the story of his life. As he'd said all she needed to know about him was that he was here now. In fact that was more than enough.

She didn't hurry back to the kitchen. She walked around the *salotto*, and ended up in front of the painting of the woman. She was standing there when Nigel came in from the hall, and kissed her good morning. She brushed his lips lightly and looked back at the painting. 'Who is she?' she asked.

'Adelanta, Contessa di Raffaele.' The name rolled off his tongue. 'Joth felt the old girl belonged here after living in the Villa for over seventy years.'

Harriet laughed, 'I wouldn't be the one to take her off the

wall, but I'd have thought he'd have hung portraits of his own family.'

'He doesn't have any relatives,' said Nigel. 'We're his family, my mother and I.'

So she had been told already, and she wasn't very interested, but she still enquired, 'How do you make that out?' and she listened intently while he told her.

'My mother knew his when they were girls. He was reared by his grandfather, a blacksmith in Yorkshire. His mother died when he was still a kid, she wasn't married, and I don't think she ever told anybody who his father was. Joth used to come down to us for the holidays.'

'That was kind of your parents,' said Harriet. She had been invited to other girls' homes for the holidays during her last years at school. 'He must have had a tough childhood,' she commented.

'I suppose so.' Nigel didn't seem too sure about that. 'He was on his own from sixteen, but nobody ever felt sorry for Joth. You always knew he was going to the top.'

'How did he get there?' She looked at the door of the study where Jotham Gaul was turning a bankrupt business into a profitable one, and regret nagged at her. She wished she could have done that. She wished there had been somebody who would have helped her to do it.

'He started as soon as he left school,' said Nigel. 'Opened a factory in the old forge, doing wrought iron stuff at first. It went like a bomb—everything Joth touches takes off. One factory led to another, although it isn't wrought iron work any more, it's heavy industry. He hasn't changed, though, he's just the same.'

'Pity, that,' said Harriet, and Nigel put both hands on her shoulders, drawing her pleadingly towards him,

'I do wish you liked him. I can't see why you two can't get on.'

'I can't see why it matters,' said Harriet, and Joth came out of the office.

'Is she telling you about her midnight fright?' he said to Nigel.

It might have seemed that Nigel was reassuring her about something, but Nigel looked blank. 'What fright?'

'The tremor,' Harriet explained. 'Didn't you feel it? I thought our volcano might be stirring. I looked up at the clouds and they looked like smoke.'

'No, it's quite safe.' Nigel smiled at her mistake. 'You do get tremors here, but it isn't this volcano.'

'So I told her last night,' said Joth, walking out of the room, and without warning Harriet felt her face flame. There was no reason why, except that Joth meant Nigel to know she had woken him in the night and that annoyed her. She said tautly, 'I went out on to the balcony and called through his window. Why didn't you warn me about the tremors?'

'I didn't think. They're very slight.' Nigel, staring thoughtfully after Joth, sounded puzzled. 'Why did you go to Joth?'

'I didn't go to anybody in particular. I went on to the balcony and his window was open. I just wanted to know if it was safe to go back to bed or if I should be down on the beach trying to hitch a lift off the island.'

'Yes, of course,' said Nigel. Her skin was suntanned and the blush hardly showed, but she could feel it scorching. She said, 'Let's get some breakfast,' and walked ahead of him but not fast enough to catch up with Jotham crossing the hall.

She was astonished that she had flushed so guiltily, and her heart had started thumping too. She could hardly have felt more flustered if she had been accused of staying in Jotham's room till morning, and she reached the kitchen almost as exasperated with herself as she was with him.

They were all downstairs by now. Alistair and Erica were at the table spreading hot rolls with melting butter and marmalade, and Annie was still at the table waiting for Nigel to come back.

When he walked in with Harriet her lips trembled and Harriet thought—she would be better for him than I would, she's got a much nicer nature. But I'm taller and thinner and I've got red hair and green eyes, and he can't see beyond the packaging.

In that moment she almost despised Nigel, and then she felt Jotham looking at her. He was talking in Italian to Elena, but when Harriet turned round she met his cynical eyes. He knew that she had noticed Annie's vulnerable face, and he was waiting, without much hope, to see if Harriet showed signs of weakening.

Not in front of you, she vowed. She slipped her slim hand, with the beautiful long nails, through Nigel's arm, and sat down beside him at table, and said sweetly, 'Croissant, darling?' She would have settled for coffee herself if Jotham hadn't said,

'Eat something, Harriet. We don't want you fainting again.'

'Fainting?' Erica echoed, but Harriet wasn't explaining that. Nor was she having Nigel telling them what Jotham meant. She bit into a croissant and enquired,

'What's on the agenda for today?'

The *festa* was. There were just under thirty islanders, but the fishing fleet would bring well over fifty guests and the feast had to be prepared. As soon as the kitchen was cleared of menfolk Elena was starting the cooking, and Erica and Annie were helping her.

The men were going out cutting greenery for the traditional decorations and Harriet would have been happy to join either party. But, as Erica reminded her, she was no use in a kitchen.

She could have been, but she had said herself that she wasn't 'signing on' as a cook, and Erica for one had no time for her. When Nigel said, 'You can come and help us cut the holly,' Annie started to say something about Harriet staying here, but Joth settled Nigel's suggestion.

'Sorry,' he said cheerfully. 'Collecting the greenery is man's work. It's a very old custom. The islanders never allow a woman along.' It might be true, although Harriet noticed that Elena looked surprised to hear it. 'Tell you what,' said Joth. 'The villa's open house on *festa* day. Why don't you do some housework? Elena's got her hands full. I'm sure she could find you a bit of light dusting.'

'Sure,' said Harriet. 'Why not? I'll do the *salotto*.'

'And the entrance hall,' said Joth.

'But of course. You want the floor scrubbed, I suppose?' She was being sarcastic there.

'Good girl,' he said approvingly. 'That's the spirit,' and both of them knew she wasn't scrubbing anything. But Nigel didn't. Nigel yelped,

'You can't scrub floors! Not with your hands.'

It wouldn't do her nails much good, but when Nigel seized her hand and held it as though it was porcelain, all she could do was pull it away and say tartly, 'Well, I wasn't proposing scrubbing with my feet,' annoyed with him for making her look such a ninny.

Nigel said no more. The men left, with secateurs and great baskets, and Elena brought ingredients out of cupboards and up from cellars. It would have been fun in the kitchen, Harriet would have loved to help, but she went into the *salotto* and dusted and polished. At the far end of the room she hesitated for a moment in front of the office door. Then she went in and dusted the chair.

There were still papers on the desk, although it all looked very tidy now. She would have liked to sit down and search for something connected with her factory, and the papers couldn't be all that private or surely Joth would have locked the door, or at least put them away in drawers. But she might not get them back in the right order, and what would she say if he walked in and caught her.

Dusting would be no excuse, and she came out of the office quickly. She wouldn't care to anger Jotham. Instinct told her that if she ever unleashed his real anger she wouldn't have time to run for cover.

She took her time over the *salotto*. Then she cleaned the hall. She did scrub the flagstones—she had to after that fuss this morning, and there were a lot of them. Half way through she stopped for lunch, and went into the kitchen where trays of little cakes and savouries were cooling and the ovens were still being emptied and refilled. It was like the kitchen of a busy hotel, and Harriet came out again with a plate of finger food and sat on a chair in the hall to eat it.

Elena would have found something for her to do in there. She had smiled at Harriet and picked out some tempting 'bites' to put on the plate, but there had been no welcome from Erica or Annie and it was easier to stay in the hall than bother with them.

By the time she had finished the flagstones she had had enough. She was hot and tired and in a filthy mood. This was her lot for the holiday. After this she'd make her bed, and do her share in the kitchen, but no more skivvying; and as for the *festa* tomorrow, she had never felt less festive in her life. She would probably spend the day in bed, and most definitely alone.

Jotham came in through the front door and she sat back on her heels and snarled, 'Get off my floor!'

He walked right across to her and said, 'I wouldn't have believed it,' and he grinned at her, and she knew that he had had a highly enjoyable day, and so had the ones in the kitchen. She was the sucker with the aching back and the broken fingernails. She looked at her hands and he said, 'The lad was right. It has ruined them.'

If she had had the strength she would have picked up the bucket of water and emptied it over him. She did the next best thing. She tipped a small dirty wave over his feet, then staggered to her own feet.

'Temper!' he reproved.

'You've seen nothing,' she told him.

'Neither have you.' But he was laughing at her and she said,

'I'm through, I'm going swimming. Is it safe to dive from the rocks that jut out past the jetty?'

'The tide's in, so it's a safe dive if you're a strong swimmer. Are you?'

'Strong enough to do the ten miles back to the mainland if I have another day like this.' She went out on to the verandah, down the wooden staircase, and scrambled along the rocks. There were plenty of footholds; it was easy to drop down on to the shelf that jutted out to sea.

She could of course have gone down to the bay and walked out, and then swum out, but she wanted to dive; and on the edge she took off her dirty cotton frock and her sandals, looked down into the deep water clear enough to see shells and weeds in the silver sand of the sea bed. Then she raised her arms, balanced on her toes for a second with the controlled poise of a ballet dancer, and went slim and straight into a perfect dive.

She touched the bottom where the water welcomed and caressed her, and she came up feeling the grime and tension floating away. She swam fast out of the bay and slowly back, happy as a child playing in a meadow, and when she looked up and saw Jotham standing on the edge of the jetty she gave him quite a friendly wave.

'It's lovely,' she called. 'Don't worry, I'm not going to cry wolf again. Look what I got last time!'

'We're going up to the temple,' he called back. 'Coming?'

'Any scrubbing to do up there?'

'No.'

'Right then, I'd like to.'

He held up a bundle. 'Here are your shoes,' and as she swam towards him he put down the bundle and walked towards the villa.

Harriet climbed out of the sea, up the steps to the jetty, put on her sandals and pulled the dress over her head. The dress was grubby, but the water had made her bra and pants almost transparent so it was as well that Joth had walked on.

He must have followed her on to the diving rock. He thought she was an idiot, show-off enough to take a header into the sea from sheer bad temper. But if she had got herself into difficulties he would have pulled her out again. When they reached shore there would have been hell to pay, but he took care of his guests, even those who were more nuisance than they were worth.

'Hey,' she called, 'wait for me!'

Joth was across the shingle at the bottom of the rock steps, and he waited and she hurried. 'Had a good day?' she asked when she reached him. 'Did you get all the greenery you wanted?'

'Yes, thank you.'

'Well, the *salotto* should be a credit, and the hall was pretty good until the water got spilt.'

He laughed and her spirits soared. She was getting the *festa* feeling. She was beginning to look forward to tomorrow, and now she wanted to see where it would all happen. She went up the rock steps ahead of him asking, 'What do the ruins look like?'

'There's very little of the barracks block,' he told her. 'Just the markings of the outer walls. But some of the pillars round the courtyard are standing. The *festa*'s held in the courtyard and around there. The temple's Mithraic.'

'So the temple itself was underground?' she said.

'That's right.' He sounded surprised that she should know that, and she went on climbing looking back at him over her shoulder.

'I have heard of Mithras,' she said. 'The soldiers' god. The Lord of Light.'

He was smiling, and she wondered if he thought she had read all this up to impress Nigel. 'You think I'm such a fool, don't you?' she said. She didn't miss her step, looking backwards, but she placed her foot on an uneven patch, and swayed slightly, and as he was immediately behind he reached out to steady her.

She was strangely conscious of his touch. As she leaned against the flat palm of his hand she felt a tingling through the wet cotton of her dress, and she gulped and said, 'One day I'll surprise you.'

She meant that one day she would prove to him that she had a brain in her head, but suddenly her head was swimming, and she stared into the grey eyes and she didn't know what she meant.

'The surprise could be mutual,' he said quietly.

'You will surprise me?' The words came out with little pauses between, and she was still pressed against his hand because she was leaning towards him as though it was necessary that she should hear what he said next and that she should go on looking at him.

'Harriet!' Her name came screaming at her. It beat on her so that she winced and closed her eyes for a moment, then she looked up at the verandah where Nigel was waving, shouting 'Harriet!' He began to walk towards the wooden steps and she called,

'All right—stay there. I'm coming!'

He waited. When she reached the top he put his arms

around her and it meant nothing at all, not a thing, but she could still feel Jotham's touch on her shoulder.

Nigel stood back. 'You're soaking!' he exclaimed.

'I've been swimming.'

'Like that?' Her dress had absorbed moisture from her skin and undies so that she did look as though she might have been in fully dressed, and she couldn't explain why she hadn't stopped to change into a swimsuit.

She said, 'It's a wonderful way of washing your clothes. A real labour-saver. We do do our own washing here don't we?' Joth nodded gravely. 'So if we all do a quick turn round the bay fully clothed every night,' said Harriet, 'there we are then.'

Nigel went on goggling. Harriet was joking, of course, she did have rather an absurd sense of humour, but what was she doing in a dripping wet dress? He looked at Joth, who said, 'I didn't push her, I just held her shoes,' and Harriet laughed and said,

'Give me five minutes. Please don't go to the temple without me.'

As she went through the hall she noticed that somebody had mopped up the puddle of dirty water she had tipped over Jotham's feet, and taken away the bucket and brushes. The floor looked really good. She didn't begrudge her scrubbing time at all.

She was downstairs again in five minutes, in dry clothes and sandals. She had washed her hair and combed it through—the sun would have to dry it—and she went with Jotham and Nigel and Annie through the olive groves that led up to the temple.

It was about fifteen minutes' climb from the villa, and there wasn't much to see until you arrived. Before the fall of Rome, when this had been an outpost at the far limit of the Roman Empire, barracks and towers would have commanded a sweeping view of the sea. But the barracks had disappeared, except for a small marked-out area of archaeological excavation.

The temple had fared better. Some of the pillars had gone and most of those that remained were broken, but the big flagstoned courtyard was almost intact, and an archway had steps that led down into darkness.

In the courtyard men and women were setting up trestle tables, garlanding the pillars with trailing creepers and wreaths of leaves, putting shrubs into tubs. Harriet didn't know anybody except Paolo, but everyone smiled at her as she wandered around.

Jotham was immediately in the middle of a busy group, but Nigel stayed with Harriet and so did Annie. They had been here before, but not for the *festa*, and they answered some of Harriet's questions. The excavations weren't a full-time project, but an archaeologist, Alexander McGregor, a friend of Joth's, was in charge of a major dig in Sardinia. He and some of his colleagues came to Piccola Licata from time to time, and stayed in the villa and worked on the dig. McGregor would be among the guests at the *festa* tomorrow.

She peered down the steps leading from the archway in the courtyard. 'There's nothing down there,' said Nigel.

'Once there must have been all sorts of things,' said Annie, 'but now it's just a big empty cave.'

The second step had a deeply cut design of two clasped hands and Harriet exclaimed delightedly, 'The Mithras sign! The clasped hands of comrades.'

'Yes,' said Nigel, and he went on talking about the traditions of the *festa*—the pairing off of the young folk, the contest of the discus throwers. Harriet hardly heard him. She was thinking that statues had vanished and pillars had cracked, but this symbol of trust had endured for twenty centuries, and she looked up slowly from the carving of the clasped hands.

She saw Jotham at once, at the other end of the court-yard, towering above everybody, the way he always did, and she thought—I trust him. If I was in danger or in trouble I would reach for his hand.

Her thoughts made her gasp, because how could a man be her enemy one day and the next seem like someone who would never harm her? She walked across the courtyard, followed by Nigel and Annie, looking at things as she went, trying out her halting Italian, all the time heading for where Jotham was unloading carboys of wine from a wagon.

He saw her coming and smiled, and she smiled and took the last few steps so quickly she was almost running. Excitement and anticipation were in the air. Everybody was in high spirits preparing for their once-a-year day. That was why she was suddenly so crazily happy, and why when she did reach him and they touched she felt the oddest sensation inside her, like an explosion of joy.

CHAPTER SEVEN

THE *festa* started for Harriet the moment she woke. She opened her eyes and right away she was filled with happiness. She couldn't remember ever feeling this way before, as though nobody could hurt her and everyone was her friend.

She dressed in a flounced white cotton skirt and a white blouse, her golden chains and her golden sandals, and hurried because she didn't want to miss a moment of the final preparations. She met Erica at the top of the stairs in a dress of Indian silk in shades of purples and pinks, and said, 'That's *beautiful*,' and Erica looked surprised.

'Well, thank you,' she said. 'You always look fantastic, of course.'

'No, I don't,' said Harriet 'and just look at my nails!' She displayed the shortened version. 'All the scrubbing yesterday. That should teach me to keep my big mouth shut,' and Erica laughed and thought that Harriet was nicer this morning.

There was a great deal to do, cartloads of food to be dragged up to the temple, by a couple of mules, and then arranged on the trestle tables that were now draped with white cloths. Elena, in her best black dress and headscarf, with a laced bodice in fine white lawn and a Spanish type black fringed shawl, was presiding over the preparations with great dignity and ordering everyone around as to the manner born.

She set Harriet to work among the baskets of freshly picked flowers, soon to wilt in the heat of the sun but first making a colourful show in bowls and vases. There were

tiny blooms of gentian blue, delicate pink and silver con-
volvulus, knapweed with big yellow heads, and a splendid
scabious with silver leaves. Harriet enjoyed her task. She
did have a talent for arranging things to advantage, and before this holiday ended she would seriously consider
Dorothy's offer of a job in the Gallery.

The men, having delivered the food, had gone down to
the harbour to wait for the fishing fleet to arrive. Tradition-
ally, the island men welcomed the visitors from the mainland ashore and conducted them through the groves up to
the temple, where the women and children were waiting for
their guests to arrive and the *festa* to begin.

Everything was set out in the courtyard when the sound
of music and singing came floating over the air, and even
Elena laughed aloud and clapped her hands. 'They are
coming!' she informed Harriet and Erica.

'Isn't it exciting?' squealed Erica. She and Harriet had
got on much better this morning. They had done a lot of
laughing, and it was exciting, listening to the singing and the
sound of guitars and tinkling bells getting louder.

'Shall we climb up the hill, then we can see them coming?' Harriet suggested, but Elena explained apologetic-
ally that it was the custom to wait, to stay here, and she
was relieved when Harriet said demurely, 'Then of course
we must wait.' Erica went into a fit of giggles—a demure
Harriet was a funny sight—and Harriet laughed and felt
her heart pounding away.

She was waiting, with a build-up of anticipation that was
almost painful. She had to force herself to stand still or she
might have run to meet him, or at least done a childish jig
of impatience.

Annie had been quiet, helping to lay the tables. Now she
was sitting on a bench, a little distance from the group, and
as Harriet looked her way Erica said, 'This isn't how she
thought it was going to be.'

Harriet couldn't very well go across and say, 'I'm not waiting for Nigel,' but Annie would soon know that, and then perhaps Annie would enjoy the *festa*.

When the procession came into sight Harriet saw that some of them were playing guitars and mandolins and clashing cymbals and that the tinkling bell-like sound was from a kind of castanet. Almost everybody was singing, a song she had never heard before, but it had a good swinging melody and she wouldn't mind dancing to it. This was certainly a way to get the party off to a flying start, and as they came trooping into the courtyard everybody seemed to run wild.

'*Saluto e benvenuto*,' the island women were saying. 'Greetings,' said Harriet, shaking hands with everybody around, including Jotham when he reached her, which he did very quickly, making straight for her.

'*Saluto*,' she said, and he dropped a hand on her shoulder and said,

'*Saluto*—you're chosen.'

'Chosen for what?' Today he was wearing a white shirt with a frilled jabot, and dark trousers. He looked very dashing, as though he should have sported a black patch over one eye.

'The unattached can choose a partner for the *festa*,' he told her gravely, and she remembered hearing about that. She saw a girl in the smiling, milling crowd put a shy hand on a young man's shoulder, several other young couples holding hands. Mostly, she guessed, they paired off with their sweethearts, but it gave the unattached a chance, and it seemed that she was Jotham's partner for the day.

Nigel came up, smiling, asking, 'How about this?' and Joth said,

'You're too late—I've chosen Harriet.'

'You're joking!' gasped Nigel.

'That's the custom,' shrugged Joth.

'Not for us, we're not locals.'

'For me. I live here—on and off.'

Nigel didn't know whether to laugh or protest. He turned to Harriet, who shrugged, keeping out of it, then he asked, 'And what am I supposed to do?'

'Find yourself another partner,' said Joth promptly.

'You mean Annie, of course.'

'That's up to you.' Joth reached for Harriet's hand and she had to trot along beside him, across the flagstones to the edge of the courtyard, beside one of the broken decorated pillars, and then he loosed her fingers.

Sprays of beech leaves were bound to the pillar by thin very strong creeper. Of course he hadn't chosen her just for the pleasure of her company, and she tucked a trailing tendril of creeper into place and said, 'You're getting me out of the running for the *festa*?'

'That's right.'

'And I'm supposed to stay with you all day?'

'You have to. They tie us together with that stuff you're playing with.'

'The *creeper*?' she screeched. 'Nobody's tying me to anybody!' Then she saw that he was laughing. 'Oh, very funny,' she said crossly. 'Any more quaint old customs?'

'The men are supposed to give the girl whatever she asks for.'

'Sounds better. What do they ask for?'

'Marriages have been arranged. It's a sort of leap-year set-up.'

'So you could be in trouble.' She grinned at him and he bent over her, whispering in her ear so that his breath tickled her cheek.

'So could you.'

'Promises, promises!' She was flirting with him, looking up through her dark lashes. It was that kind of day, it was fun. 'Didn't anyone ask you to marry them last year?' He had been here last year. 'Surely you had a partner?' she said.

'Of course I had a partner.' Joth had glamorous girl-friends. Who else had been here? she wondered. Perhaps in the room she had now, opening on to the balcony, and she felt a pang of something very like jealousy.

'And there she is,' said Joth, and raised a hand in beam-ing salute to a very fat jolly-looking woman, well past middle age. 'Her name's Mafalda and she's a widow.'

Harriet could imagine the merry widow, the life and soul of the party, tapping the new Signore on the shoulder. Mafalda looked like a lady who liked a joke, and Harriet was delighted to see her. 'And her request wasn't a hus-band?' she said with dancing eyes.

'As I recall,' said Jotham solemnly, 'she wanted a goat,' and Harriet shrieked with laughter, clapping a hand to her mouth. 'I'm not saying a word,' she said, in muffled tones.

'You'd better not,' said Joth.

Nigel was standing with Erica and Alistair, watching the musicians forming into a group around the archway that led down into the old temple, when Annie walked up to him. He hadn't gone to her, but she reached him and put her hand on his arm, and then Harriet remembered what Annie had said, about getting engaged at the *festa*.

'She wouldn't, would she?' said Harriet, alarmed.

Joth was looking at them too, and his voice was very quiet. 'Wouldn't what?'

'Ask him to marry her.' There were people moving be-tween, she could only get glimpses of them, but obviously Annie had claimed Nigel as her partner. 'We mustn't let her!' Harriet took a step forward and Joth's hand closed round her wrist, holding her where she stood.

'Why should we stop her?' The eyes were hard again, and he thought she was thinking of herself.

She said, 'Because he's more than likely to turn her down.'

'Then she'll be no worse off.'

'But she *will*. She'll be hurt. Annie couldn't shrug off a rejection like that. She'd be shattered.'

He was still holding her wrist, but now his grip was a gentle pressure. 'She isn't stupid,' he said. 'She wouldn't propose marriage unless she thought that was what he wanted as well, and she knows it isn't. But let her have to-day. She was promised this before you turned up.'

It was something to have Jotham pleading. He had a persuasive charm that was hard to resist, and in this case Harriet had no choice. 'I hope for her sake that you know her as well as you think you do,' she said tartly. 'You're certainly putting yourself out to see she enjoys her day. She might have done better to pick you.'

'What the hell would she do with me?' he asked. 'Or come to that, what could I do with her?' and she felt her lips twitching and murmured,

'Perhaps Nigel is more her cup of tea.'

Jotham smiled, as well he might. That was the sort of thing he wanted to hear her say, but she had enjoyed hearing that his admiration for Annie was limited.

'Talking of tea,' he said, 'may I get you a glass of wine?'

She waited by the pillar while he went across to where the wine was being poured from barrels and carboys. The musicians were playing now, but everybody went on chattering and laughing and calling across to their friends. Jotham soon returned, through the crowd, holding two glasses high.

The wine tasted young and raw and made Harriet blink when she swallowed. 'Is it to your taste?' he asked, and she laughed. The sun was hot and there was colour everywhere. The older women were in basic black, but the younger ones wore bright dresses with flounces and sequins. It was a dazzling scene, all colour and music and gaiety.

She looked around and then up at the man beside her and nodded. 'Is it to your taste?' she asked, and he looked at her. Just at her, as though they were quite alone. 'Very much so,' he said, and her heart leapt in her throat.

'Introduce me to the lady, laddie,' said a very short wiry man who had suddenly materialised, and Harriet didn't need to be told that this was McGregor the archaeologist. He said he was delighted to meet her, shaking her hand enthusiastically. 'We redheads should stick together.' He had flaming red hair and beard and his skin was tanned terracotta.

'Not this redhead,' said Joth, putting an arm around her. 'This one sticks close to me.'

It was all joking, but she felt fine, close to Joth. She liked the light weight of his arm across her back, his hand cupping her shoulder. 'Och, I tell you, lassie, he's a terrible feller,' said McGregor. 'You should pay no heed at all to anything he says.'

'I know,' she said. 'I know.'

Everybody there thought she was Jotham's girl. Except Nigel and Annie and Erica and Alistair, of course. There were knowing looks and smiles as they strolled around the courtyard and selected food from the tables, and settled down to eat—picnic fashion—with Erica and Alistair, using the plinth of a broken pillar as a table.

The music played all the time, most of the time the square was full of dancers and occasionally a singer burst into song. Harriet found the music and the sunshine as intoxicating as the wine. She hummed along with the choruses, although she didn't know a word of the songs, and swayed with the dancers, sitting on a flagstone, her feet tucked under her.

After a while Nigel and Annie came over with a plate of sticky cakes, a dish of savouries and a jug of wine, and

Annie asked, 'Is there room?'

Of course there was, miles of it. Nigel sat down as near as he could get to Harriet and Annie sat down by Erica and ate a cake very slowly, looking into the distance as though she was listening to the music.

'That was a dirty trick of Joth's taking you off like that,' said Nigel while Joth was talking to somebody else, and Harriet shrugged,

'Forget it. Isn't it a nice party?'

'You seem to be enjoying yourself.' Nigel didn't sound too pleased, and she said,

'Shouldn't I be?'

Jotham turned round then and Nigel didn't answer her question, and the picnic went on until suddenly the music stopped and there was a great clash of cymbals that made Harriet nearly jump out of her skin.

The discus throwing was about to start. 'If it was a beauty contest,' Nigel announced, 'there wouldn't be any contest. Harriet would be the winner, of course.'

'Nonsense,' she said, briskly, and wished he would shut up. 'What's happening?' she asked.

McGregor had joined them by now and he explained what was fairly obvious, that the winner would be the man who threw the discus farthest. The discus was a stone with a hole in the middle, which had been carried out into the centre of the courtyard. A man was carefully drawing a large circle round it in chalk and everybody was moving to this end of the square.

'It was originally used for hunting,' said McGregor, and several men came out of the crowd and Jotham got to his feet.

'Come on,' he urged Nigel and Alistair. 'Give it a go.'

'All right,' said Alistair.

'I'm not making a fool of myself,' said Nigel, and Annie nodded agreement.

Most of the men wore coloured scarves, some round their necks, some tied round their upper arms, the women were putting them on, and Harriet cried, 'They're the head-scarves! They're wearing their ladies' favours.'

'Hang on,' said Erica, and she took off the fine silk scarf that matched her dress and fastened it neatly round Alistair's waist in a cummerbund.

'Definitely me,' said Alistair, and Harriet wished she had worn a scarf or had something she could pin on Joth, who was asking her,

'What are you going to give me to take into battle?'

'This,' she said, and she jumped up and kissed him. It was an impulsive friendly gesture, a kiss like that meant nothing. She was laughing, they were all laughing—except Nigel—but the feel of his cheek against her lips stirred her so that if no one had been looking on she would have stopped laughing and asked herself, What on earth is happening to me?

But there was no time for introspection. Jotham and Alistair got a roar of approval as they walked over to join the competitors. Jotham Gaul had provided most of the food and drink today, so he was a popular figure already, and Alistair was being cheered for joining in, and for wearing his lady's favour according to custom.

Then utter silence fell and the first man stepped forward and picked up the discus, lifting it high over his left shoulder and down to the right, almost to the ground, up and down a couple of times, then whirling round within the circle of chalk and letting fly.

The discus went over a broken pillar at the far end of the square, skimming like a bird, landing in the rough grass. A man ran out with a marker on a pointed stick and forced the marker into the ground. The distance was measured and announced, and a cheer went up while Erica muttered,

'I hope they don't knock down another pillar with that thing!'

'Or hit anybody,' Harriet whispered. The crowd was behind the throwers, but the whirling around could disorientate anybody who was new to the game, and the discus was stone and looked heavy. When Alistair was ushered forward the girls held their breath. Alistair did the lifting up and bending down slowly but correctly, then he staggered round and a howl went up of good-humoured catcalls and jeers. He only threw the discus a short distance, not even to the end of the courtyard, and came back shaking his head and grinning while the booing went on, with slow handclaps and wide smiles all around.

'Disqualified!' he groaned, collapsing on the ground.

'What did you do?' squealed Erica. 'How could you get disqualified before you'd even thrown it?'

'Stepped out of the circle. That's as bad as slugging the referee.' He put his head in his hands, pretending to be downcast. 'Well, it's up to Joth now—I've let the side down. Sorry, folks.'

A dozen other men came forward, went through identical motions, and hurled the discus as their hunting forefathers had done; there was poetry and skill and strength in the age-old ritual, and Harriet was caught in the spell of it. After each throw there was cheering, derisory if the cast fell short, prolonged after a good performance.

When Joth stepped into the circle they cheered him before he had even picked up the discus and Alistair shouted, 'Mind where you're putting your feet!'

Joth gave them the boxer's salute, raised clasped hands, and nobody was taking this seriously. There wasn't the silence for him. The ripple of laughter went on, and he picked up the discus, lifted it up and down, once, twice. Unlike Alistair, there was nothing jerky about his move-

ments. When he whirled round fast and threw hard the
laughter stopped as all eyes watched the flight of the discus.
It was a good throw, out among the leading markers, and
then the applause was generous and genuine, and Alistair
whistled, 'How did he do it?'

'Does anybody know anything Joth can't do?' said Nigel,
as though he begrudged the cheering.

'Can't say as I do,' said McGregor cheerfully, and they
all, but Nigel, clapped vigorously as Joth came back to join
them.

'Have you been practising?' Harriet asked.

'Sheer luck.' He sat down beside her.

Luck had played a part, but he had learned from watching and he had the strength. His broad powerful shoulders
had split his shirt at the moment of hurling the discus and
they laughed again when Annie pointed that out. 'You can't
go round like that,' said Annie, and Harriet was sure she
was going to offer to mend it, although Joth was unlikely to
wear a shirt that was stitched all up the back.

He took it off now and said, 'Better?' About a third of
the men were stripped to the waist in the heat of the day,
and Harriet reflected that she had been wrong about him
being overweight. He was hard muscle, and she had a sudden urge to run her fingers along the smooth brown skin
of his shoulder or even to press her lips to it.

'And you can give me my favour back,' Erica teased.
'Getting disqualified!' She undid her scarf from around his
waist and Alistair grinned, and Joth looked at Harriet,

'Do you want your favour returned?'

She tried to smile and say, 'Yes, please,' because that
was what everyone expected her to say, and then Joth would
kiss her, smiling, and it would all be a joke. But she said,
'It must have been lucky for you as you did so well, so
you'd better keep it,' and it wasn't because she couldn't
bear him to touch her, as it would have been only a little

while ago. It was because the thought of him kissing her set up a sweet racing panic in her blood. But not in front of them all.

Some time she would ask for her favour back, she promised herself, and smiled, and felt as though she was hugging a lovely secret.

Joth's throw brought him in fourth, and that was unheard-of for a beginner. Paolo, the runner-up, said that with a little practice the Signore would make a champion, and McGregor grunted in Harriet's ear, 'The laddie's daft, telling him to practise—Joth'll be beating him next year. If Jotham's throwing he's going to throw further than anyone else or be knowing the reason why. Like I told you lassie, he's a man to watch, a terrible feller.'

Nigel had said years ago that Jotham was a man to watch, it seemed to be a general opinion. Harriet chuckled, 'But don't you think he's worth watching?' and McGregor agreed, 'He is that,' and there was no mistaking the real regard that the wiry little Scot had for Jotham Gaul.

It was a halcyon day. Several times Harriet thought, I shall remember this day for the rest of my life. The music and dancing went on and when the picnic was over she asked Joth, 'Shall we dance?'

'Sorry, I can't dance,' he apologised.

'You see,' she said to Nigel, 'there is something he can't do,' and Nigel said,

'That doesn't matter, though, does it?' telling them all, 'Harriet's a solo performer. She doesn't need anybody else when she dances.'

The dancers in the courtyard were probably all couples, but most of the young ones were stepping out separately. 'Is it permitted to dance alone?' asked Harriet. 'I wouldn't want to go against tradition.'

'Feel free,' said Joth. 'So long as I don't lose sight of you.'

'What happens if you do?'

'Then I come and find you.'

She laughed, and danced, under the hot sun, to the music of the guitar and the mandolins. She had never felt freer or happier, and most of the zinging joy of the dance came from looking at Joth and seeing him smile, and coming back when she was too hot to dance any longer, and finding him waiting for her. She was having the time of her life, and she hoped that everyone else was too.

Most of them certainly were, but Annie and Nigel looked rather out of things. They just sat and watched, and talked, but as Alistair put it, 'In no way are those two having a ball.' By mid-afternoon Annie had developed a headache in the heat and Nigel had said he would take her back to the Villa.

Harriet was slowly working her way through all the dishes, trying everything, and washing it down with orange juice, lemonade, and occasional gulps of wine. All the time Joth was with her. They went with McGregor down into the dark cave that had been the temple, and walked over the area where the barracks had stood. Harriet was fascinated by it all, and she listened with complete concentration to a little history lesson.

'I envy you,' she said. 'Who knows what you'll find?'

McGregor smiled. 'Not much buried treasure. Anything of value went long ago.'

'But it must be marvellous, stepping back thousands of years, knowing how it was.' For a moment she saw the towers and the walls, and she laughed a little self-consciously because she was over-romanticising. 'I know it's mostly just very hard work.'

'He can always use help,' said Joth. 'When they come over some time why don't you take another holiday here?'

'I'd like that.' McGregor was nodding as though the suggestion had his approval. 'If I could arrange it I'd love to sign on with your digging team.' She turned to Joth. 'How about you?'

'If you come,' he said, 'and if I can manage it, I shall certainly be here.' He didn't say anything about any of the others. He only looked at her, as if this was only between them.

All day long there was feasting and music and dancing. The *festa* always lasted until night fell, when the visitors would leave for home, winding in a procession of bobbing lights down to the harbour. But in the early evening the party was going as merrily as ever, although Harriet felt that soon Jotham might suggest returning to the Villa. Nigel and Annie hadn't come back and now Alistair and Erica had said they were calling it a day.

'Where do you find the energy?' Erica asked Harriet. 'Every time I've seen you you've been dancing or dashing around, but you still look fresh as a daisy.'

Until today almost everything Erica had said to Harriet had been caustic, but she smiled when she said that. Erica was friendlier. Everybody had been friendly. It had been the most wonderful day, and Harriet wondered what would happen if she said, 'So long as I show that I'm enjoying every minute Joth might let me stay until the visitors leave. I don't want the *festa* to end, because so long as it lasts we are partners, he and I.'

She wouldn't say that, of course. She said, 'I'll be tired tomorrow, but I don't want to leave yet.' But when, a few minutes later, she sat down on a bench and Joth sat down beside her, she was sure he was going to say, 'Are you ready to go?' Perhaps that he had work waiting in his office, or just that they would be more comfortable in easy chairs down in the Villa. After all they had been at the *festa* since early morning.

She had to do something to stop him saying that, and she

looked up at the volcano and asked, 'Is it possible to climb to the top?'

'Yes, but not this late. It has its hazards.' Then he added, 'Although we could walk a little way if you liked.'

Harriet was on her feet at once. She wasn't tired. She believed she could have climbed to the summit, but she accepted that that would have been dangerous as soon as the light began to fail. They walked out of the courtyard, past the site of the barracks, and up through the terraced groves, climbing steadily.

The noise of the *festa* went with them and they hardly talked at all. She would have chattered away with anyone else, but she walked quietly with Joth, and yet she felt that she was getting to know him better all the time, as though they were sharing not only scents and sounds but thoughts and emotions. They didn't have to talk. With a smile and a look they were communicating without words.

The night was so beautiful, the day had been fabulous, but she didn't have to go on about it. Jotham knew that she was happy, that everything was just about perfect. She had never had real rapport with any human being before, there had always been something in her that stayed aloof, but not tonight. Tonight she would have trusted this man whom she had disliked so heartily, so recently, with her life.

It wasn't hard climbing yet, if you were young and strong. He didn't offer to help her over the rugged patches. She was up as easily as he, and enjoying the effort. Above the terraces they passed beech trees and black pines, and then they reached a small plantation of silver firs.

Here the grass seemed mosslike, and softer than the hard unsheltered ground they had been scaling. It was springy underfoot and they turned and looked back, down to the courtyard of the temple. There was still enough light to see the people, and lamps had been lit here and there—

carbine lamps brought up from the boats. You could still hear the music.

This was Joth's land, it was practically his island. Harriet began, 'This holiday development——'

'Don't worry,' he said. 'The villa may be adapted to take visitors. Any other buildings will fit into the countryside. There won't be many of them. I'm not out to make a quick killing. Nothing will be spoiled, I promise you.'

Harriet was so glad that she couldn't speak for a moment and he said, 'That was what you wanted to hear, wasn't it?'

'Yes,' she said. 'That nothing would be spoiled. Yes.'

She could feel his eyes on her and she lifted her head and the colour came into her cheeks. Suddenly she was shy. Harriet Brookes, the sophisticated cosmopolitan, blushing like a schoolgirl because a man was going to take her into his arms.

She had never felt this way before. Plain scared, so that she instinctively backed away, and when a lively tune floated up she found herself moving to the music, doing a careful spin or two.

Joth looked amused, and she knew she was being ridiculous. 'Dancing, swimming, driving too fast,' he said. 'You're a restless girl.'

She snapped her fingers, swaying, smiling, 'No more restless than you.'

But he had an inner core of quiet strength. He would never get into a car and put his foot down and go fast, heading for nowhere, much less have to whirl around dancing to shed his inhibitions. There was no comparison between them and she knew it, and he came to her and took both her hands, and she tried to tug them away. He stood still and she was trembling.

'Rest now,' he said, and she stopped pulling away from him, and they sat down where the hill rose behind them and you could lean back against the soft moss, and she was trembling again. He began to stroke her hair and she whispered, 'No,' because it was too sudden, the physical attraction was too strong. She needed time to think, to decide.

'It's been a good day,' he said, and she knew he wasn't going to make love to her yet. They were going to be like this for a while, him stroking her hair, her nestled close beside him. Nothing was going to happen that might rush her into a commitment, and then she relaxed with a deep contented sigh.

She was tired. She was so weary and she hadn't realised it until now, and she yawned and laughed, 'I've eaten too much. It was a superb spread. What did you think of the flower arrangements? I did those.'

'Very colourful,' he said. With her head on his shoulder his voice seemed to rumble in the barrel of his chest. He was wearing a red and blue checked shirt that Elena had had brought up to the *festa* from the villa. It had offended her sense of propriety that the Signore should walk around stripped to the waist like a peasant. Joth had laughed and said, 'But I am a peasant,' and Elena had frowned, with a little shake of the head. She was having none of that.

Harriet sat up and traced round a couple of squares on his collar bone with a fingertip and said, 'You're not colour-blind, are you?'

'No. Why?'

'I've wondered. Some of the clothes you wear.'

Joth chuckled, 'I'm not colour-blind, but I don't have much colour sense.'

'That accounts for it.' She dropped her head back again on his shoulder. 'I have a terrific colour sense,' she said. 'Not much common sense sometimes, but a fantastic colour sense.' She closed her eyes and went on talking. 'There's this art gallery I have a very small share in. Well, it's a very small gallery, but it puts on some good exhibitions. Anthony's work went on show there.'

'I saw the photograph,' said Joth.

'So you said.' A photograph in the local newspaper of the opening of the exhibition, with Harriet standing beside Anthony. She had been fond of Anthony, but never at peace with him like this. 'I've been asked to work there full time,' she said.

'I'm sure you'd be a success.' If he meant that, she wondered if she might ask him for a job in the factory some time.

She said, 'I wish I'd known about the state of the family business.'

'You'd have done something about it?'

'Yes, I'm sharp. I learn quickly.'

Before her father died she had played around, but if he had ever shown signs of needing her help she would have worked herself to death for him. But her father had never bothered to face facts. He had relied on his charm and his luck, and luck had stayed with him until he drew his last breath.

Life was like that for some. She said, 'Nigel says that everything prospers for you. Always has done and no sweat.'

'Nigel,' said Joth drily, 'doesn't have a clue. I've sweated every inch of the way. Blood half the time. And tears.' He smiled at her, lying in the crook of his arm. 'The tears were a long time ago.'

'When you were young?'

'Very.'

'That was when I did my crying,' she said. They shared a memory of loneliness for a moment, and she felt the slow strong beat of his heart, and the warmth of the strong arm that enfolded her, and she thought—we shall never be lonely again.

'I'm so tired.' This time she couldn't stop yawning. 'I

danced myself to a standstill.'

'About time too.' His lips touched her hair. 'Be quiet,' he said, and Harriet was quiet. She wanted to stay here and rest, because in no arms and no bed had she ever known such peace. Soon she was sleeping like a child.

When she woke she knew at once where she was, and that was odd because her sleep had been deep and dreamless, but she woke in Joth's arms with no astonishment at all. She had his shirt around her and she lay close to him and the music had stopped.

Either he had been awake looking at her, or her stirring had disturbed him, because he smiled when she turned her head towards him and said, 'Hello.'

'What's the time?' She wasn't wearing her watch. Joth leaned across her to check his—her head had been pillowed on his arm—and said, 'Just after three.'

'In the *morning*?' That was a silly question, with the stars out so brightly and the moon up there. She must have slept for hours, and she sat up and looked down at the silent scene and asked, 'Where did they all go?'

'To bed.'

'You should have woken me.'

'Why? You were tired.' So he had let her sleep, and stayed with her. He was kind and caring and there weren't too many like that about. In fact she had never met another like him. She was stiff for a second or two when she got to her feet and she held on to his arm. 'I'm still half asleep, still dopey.'

'Take your time,' he said.

When she flexed her shoulders the shirt draped over her slipped away, and she caught it and handed it to him, smiling. 'You'd better put this on. Elena doesn't like you walking around like a peasant.'

'Who's going to tell her?' He knotted the arms of the shirt around his neck, and in the moonlight the hard rippling muscles of his body were as beautiful as a Greek statue's. He would laugh if she told him he was beautiful, he wouldn't believe her. But if he made love to me now, she thought, the earth would shake and I should think it was the volcano.

'Come on,' he said. He was taking her home, and she looked back regretfully. She said, 'You're sure it's safe, the volcano?'

'Yes.' His arm was around her, he was helping her down although she had climbed up on her own. Of course it was riskier by moonlight, you couldn't see so well. 'But what is pretty spectacular round here are the storms,' he said. 'We have the best storms.'

'Perhaps you'd lay one on for me some time?'

'You come back and we'll see.'

They smiled at each other and Harriet knew that she would come back. 'Tell me about your storms,' she said.

'The first time I thought the end of the world had come. It had been very still. And hot. Hotter than usual with no air, everybody gasping for breath.'

It was warm even now, but there was a light breeze blowing. She could imagine how it would be before a storm when you were literally gasping for air. It would feel like the beginning of the end of the world.

Joth went on, 'The storms come suddenly. The sun can still be shining over there, but suddenly the clouds are on you and you're plunged into darkness. It's hell let loose. Not so much the wind as the rolling thunder, and you get these tremendous flashes of lightning in great jagged sheets. When it strikes the sea the water hisses, and if it hits the ground you can hear the burning and crackling and smell the sulphur.'

He held her hand as she slid down a little incline. 'I guarantee you,' he said. 'You want the best storms, we've got 'em.'

'How do you think the tourists will like them?' It sounded a fantastic spectacle, but it also sounded terrifying.

'I was thinking of billing them as one of the attractions,' he announced solemnly. 'Like the Blackpool illuminations,' and she chortled.

'Ah, but then if they don't get one they could complain they'd been cheated. I don't suppose even you can actually switch them on.'

'I'm working on it.'

'Nigel,' she said, 'will expect you to have cracked the problem before the brochures go out, because everything's easy for you.'

They passed the place where the barracks had been, and in the silence she whispered, 'Are they still on guard?'

'Who knows?' Joth hissed back. By moonlight Harriet could imagine it again as it might have been, when the guardians of the island had kept watch here in tall towers. She would come back and help on the dig, and Joth would come, and they would share in the work and the discoveries.

They passed the deserted courtyard, littered with the debris of the *festa*. The flowers were dead and the greenery hung limp around the pillars. Tomorrow everything would be swept away and another year would pass before the music struck up again. But it had been a memorable day. She would remember every minute of it.

She said, 'I hope Mithras enjoyed his *festa*.'

'That was the feast of Santa Maria dei Greci,' Joth intoned, and Harriet laughed.

'Well, I hope she enjoyed it too. I know I did.'

They were walking with linked hands and Joth's fingers tightened around hers in a warm and steady clasp. Like the entwined hands on the step she thought. Trust. And she knew that she would walk anywhere with this man.

They went through the groves towards the villa, with no sounds but the soft soughing of the sea and the light whisper of the breeze. She was beginning to feel tired again. It was good not to have to talk, to walk quietly home, her hand in Joth's.

There were no lights burning in the villa, and as he opened the door she whispered, 'Everybody's in bed. What do you think they thought had happened to us?'

Joth grinned, 'Not that you'd fallen asleep,' and she put a hand over her mouth, as though she might wake the household if she laughed aloud.

'I shouldn't think many girls fall asleep when they're out with you, do they?' He laughed and she thought, I'm jealous of them, whoever they are. But they're not here, and I am, so why should I worry?

At the top of the stairs all the doors were closed. The house felt as though everyone was asleep, and Harriet went on tiptoe, although she might as well not have bothered as Joth didn't.

Outside her door she whispered, 'Goodnight?' It was a question really, but he said,

'Goodnight. What's left of it.' He stood looking down at her as though he knew that she was very tired, more understanding than anyone else had ever been, and she said,

'It's tomorrow, isn't it? What shall we do tomorrow? After we've tidied up the courtyard.'

'You and I will think of something.' He didn't touch her, not even to kiss her, but again she felt the lovely warm glow of happiness as if she was still lying in his arms on the hillside.

She said huskily, 'Yes, I think we might,' then she opened the door and went into her own room, because if she had stayed with him any longer she would have said, 'But it is tomorrow,' and she would have reached for him.

Moonlight filled her room. There were no shutters up here and no one had drawn the blinds. She kicked off her sandals, as soon as she closed the door, and went across to the window, with the little balcony outside and the volcano filling the sky.

She was almost too weary to move. She had to undress and wash, she was sticky and dirty and her hair—when she lifted heavy hands to it—was full of bits of moss. But she felt more like dropping on the bed as she was and going out like a light.

She heard the movement, as she turned from the window, and croaked, 'Who's that?'

Then Nigel spoke, getting up from a divan chair against the wall. 'Well, it worked, didn't it?' he said savagely. 'It all worked out just as he planned it.'

CHAPTER EIGHT

'PLANNED what?' said Harriet.

'To get you away from me.' Nigel's voice was ragged.
In the white moonlight that filled the room he looked pale,
his hair dishevelled, and Harriet felt bone weary. It was
almost too much effort to talk. She began,

'I am very tired——' and Nigel laughed harshly.

'That doesn't surprise me!'

'We went for a walk,' she tried to explain. 'Climbing up,
past the groves, and then we sat down and I fell asleep.'

'For God's sake!' he jeered, and it did sound a lame
tale, but it happened to be the truth and she said wearily,

'Oh, go to bed, do, I can't deal with you tonight.'

'That would be asking rather a lot, even with your
stamina.' Harriet let the double-meaning pass. He couldn't
have had a comfortable wait, sitting in a chair, fuming with
jealousy.

'How long have you been here?' Harriet asked, but when
he said,

'Hours!' sounding as aggrieved as though she had invited him and then stayed out half the night she snapped,

'Well, more fool you!' Her head was starting to ache,
but she apologised for that, 'I'm sorry, but I don't care
for surprises like this.' She had wanted to go quietly to
bed. She had known that her dreams would have been
good, and the sooner she fell asleep the sooner it would
be morning. She couldn't start explaining or apologising to
Nigel, she just didn't have the strength, and in any case
there was nothing to apologise for and nothing to explain.

She went across to the dressing table and slumped on the

stool, then put her elbows on the table and her head in her hands. 'Please go away,' she begged.

'If I don't what will you do?' Nigel was behind her. If she lifted her head she would see his dim reflection in the mirror. 'Shout for Joth?'

'No.' She felt the faint throbbing of her temples against the palms of her hands. The last thing she wanted was a rumpus at this hour, disturbing the household. It wasn't her fault Nigel was waiting for her, Joth would know that. But she was sorry for Nigel and she wasn't making things worse for him by shrieking for help.

'He's a great one for helping, he's a good friend, is Joth,' said Nigel with what was probably irony, and she said,

'Yes,' very quietly.

'But he had his priorities, and top of the list is my mother. Joth would do anything for her.'

A picture came into Harriet's mind of Joth crossing to where Sylvia Joliffe sat at that breakfast table in Tudor House, tears streaming down her cheeks. He had looked at Harriet then as though he could have struck her because she seemed to be laughing while Sylvia wept. 'She was his mother's friend, and his mother didn't have many friends after Joth was born,' said Nigel. 'Unmarried mothers didn't, thirty years ago.'

That was good of Sylvia Joliffe, brave and kind. Harriet admired her for that and wished that Nigel's mother could have been her friend.

'She's worried about you,' Nigel went on. 'She wants Joth to put a stop to it.'

Harriet had been told that plainly enough before she came here, and Sylvia Joliffe was right to be worried because Annie would be better for Nigel than Harriet. Annie loved him.

'And that's what Joth is doing now,' said Nigel.

That was what was happening, but it was no longer a deliberate course of action. It was just happening, like yesterday had happened, one thing following another, naturally and marvellously. 'Well, yes,' she said, 'but——'

'Oh, he fancies you,' said Nigel. 'Of course he does. But he's splitting us up, that's what he's doing. He's showing me I couldn't hold you and I suppose he's right. But you won't hold Joth for long, because he doesn't even like you.'

She had raised her head and now she felt the muscles in her face stiffen so that her reflection looked like a mask in pale smooth stone. Joth hadn't liked her. He had disliked everything about her, and told her so. He'd thought she was greedy and grasping, selfish and superficial, and she couldn't be sure he'd changed his opinion of her. Why should he have done?

He'd chosen her for his partner at the *festa* to keep her away from Nigel, to give Annie her chance. He hadn't chosen Harriet because he liked her, although it had been a good day. She said, 'He's going to a lot of trouble.'

'What trouble?' Nigel demanded scornfully. 'He's having a bloody good time.'

That was possible. It was no hardship for a red-blooded man to be in the company of a pretty girl. He didn't have to like her, especially if he had a friend who might make a fool of himself over this girl and here was a way of showing that she would always play for the highest stakes.

Harriet could just have walked into a neat little trap, but she didn't want to believe it. Her eyes were dark in the stillness of her face, and she tried to smile, but her lips wouldn't move. She felt as though she was turning into stone.

Nigel said, 'Before the *festa* he was talking about Annie and saying I'd be a fool if I got myself landed with a girl like you,' and something exploded in her brain.

Their voices came roaring at her down the years ....
'You're not landing me with Harriet!' Her mother and her
father, each terrified that they might be left with the
daughter they despised. 'You can get out and you can take
Harriet with you.' 'Don't think you're landing me with
Harriet!' She had heard that, over and over it seemed,
huddled on a staircase or lying on a bed, her hands over
her ears. And now a burning flame wrapped her from
head to foot, shame and rejection and anger, so that she
leapt to her feet, whirling round on Nigel, her eyes blazing and the swirl of her red hair bright as fire in the grey
shadows of the room.

'How dare he? How dare you? Get out of my sight!'
Her voice was low, but Nigel gasped and blinked and
stammered,

'I'm sorry, but I've had a hellish day.'

He was repeating what Joth had said, there was no
forgetting that. But it wasn't Nigel's fault and she said,
'Poor Nigel,' although right now she couldn't feel sorry
for anybody, not with these voices inside her ripping open
the old deep wounds.

'You're the most beautiful girl in the world,' said Nigel
huskily.

'Am I?' That was nonsense. If she turned on the light
she would look dirty and tired and haggard, and probably
a hundred years old. 'I'm crazy about you,' said Nigel, and
she snapped,

'How long for?'

'Always.'

Oh no, she thought, only so long as I stay smooth-
skinned and glossy-haired, and she laughed a little and
asked, 'Is this a marriage proposal?'

'Yes,' he said, very fast although she didn't believe for
a moment that he had meant to ask her to marry him just
yet. He had been manoeuvered into it, as she had been

set up earlier, and that should have been amusing. 'It is, yes,' he said, and she said,

'Thank you, that's nice. And rather sudden. Do you mind if I sleep on it?' She opened her door and smiled at him, and he went out because he couldn't think what else he could do.

He *was* crazy about Harriet. He had had a wretched day, watching her with Joth, and it had got worse, waiting and imagining all these hours after everyone else had gone to bed and they weren't back. Or if they were back Harriet wasn't sleeping in her own room.

God knows he wanted her. He supposed that meant he wanted to marry her. He supposed he should have said more than just, 'Yes.' He should have taken her in his arms and kissed her and shown her that he was crazy about her. But Harriet was a strange girl. He couldn't keep his eyes off her, but most of the time he hadn't a clue what was going on in her head. Even if they married he didn't know whether he would ever understand her.

As it happened Harriet had no intention of marrying him. She saw, far more clearly than he, that marriage between them would be a hopeless situation. Although before she came to the island she had been prepared to consider it.

In the morning she would tell him that it wouldn't work, and he would be relieved that she wasn't holding him to his impetuous offer, because in his heart he must know that Joth was right, that he would be a fool to get himself landed with a girl like Harriet. That was Jotham Gaul's opinion, and Jotham was never wrong.

She could have wept, but her days of weeping were over. Tears were for children, although she was feeling as desolate now as she had done when she was a child. She turned the key in the door and went to the window and fastened the latch and let down the blind. There was no risk of Jotham coming along the balcony, but she wanted everything locked, everybody kept out. The only time you were really safe was when no one could get at you.

She had to feel her way in darkness for the wall switch, and the light dazzled her for a moment. She stood with closed eyes, the light pressing like thumbs on her lids and the ache filling her head.

All the things Joth had said before they came here came back to her ... 'Don't get any ideas about marrying Nigel' ... 'I wouldn't touch you with a barge pole' ... Except, of course, to stop her marrying Nigel, because for Nigel she was very bad news.

Her heart was pounding and she was shaking, the way it used to be when rage was her only weapon, an eruption of frustration and fury. If Jotham had been in the room she would have screamed at him, or more likely struck out. She ran to the window and opened it with fumbling fingers. She wanted to get into his room and tell him just what she thought of him, and ask what gave him the right to warn Nigel against getting landed with her, as though no man in his right mind would want to be with Harriet Brookes for long.

But before she could step on to the balcony common sense hit her. She couldn't run around screaming in the middle of the night. She was a grown woman, not a child, she had to show some self-control. She had to keep her anger in this room, with the doors locked; and she closed the window again.

Then she picked up her hairbrush and brushed her hair hard, dragging out the tiny scraps of moss that were entangled in it. She stripped and washed and the flare of anger subsided into a seething resentment. Oh, she was angry still, but she wouldn't be throwing anything at anybody. Except words, perhaps. She would have plenty to say to Jotham Gaul if he was still playing the idiot game of protecting Nigel from her.

And he was, of course. Nothing had happened to make him change his opinion of her in the last few days. Nothing that Nigel had just said should have surprised her. She couldn't think why it had, because she'd known it all.

She should be getting into bed now, but she was as wakeful as though it was midday, her mind so alert that her body's weariness seemed to have vanished. She would have liked to go down to the beach and swim out for a long way, but climbing down the rock steps might be tricky, and she wasn't risking a broken leg or a sprained ankle, or anything that might confine and keep her here.

Besides, if she went out someone might hear, and come after her. Jotham perhaps, and she couldn't have faced him again tonight for a thousand pounds. From wanting to get to him, and scream at him, she had rapidly reached the stage of wishing profoundly that she need never set eyes on him again.

She had brought a couple of novels with her and she read one of them for a while. Then she wrote a few letters. She described the island, and the Villa and the *festa*, in almost identical glowing terms in all of them. But on Dorothy's letter she added, 'The man I told you about did ask me to marry him, an hour or two ago. I'm sure he regretted it at once because it would be an almighty mistake for the pair of us. I hope he did, because no way am I saying yes. But the job you talked about, in the Gallery, now that's different. I would like to try that, please, and I'd like to start as soon as I get back.'

That was her future settled for a while. She wanted the job. She was sure she would be happy in it, and she thought she might make a success of it, but right now she had no enthusiasm for anything. She felt completely apathetic, although she was still putting off getting into bed. But when she saw light through the slatted blind, and knew that dawn was breaking, she slipped between the sheets and shut her eyes and tried to keep her mind a blank.

She had known the nightmare would come. It usually did on bad nights, hardly varying. She never knew how long they lasted, but this time, when she woke, she seemed to have relived all her years as an unwanted child. She lay breathing shallowly, engulfed in misery, and even when she got out of bed she couldn't throw off the black depression.

It was late, but nobody had called her. She was surprised that Nigel hadn't knocked on her door. Or was she? She was supposed to be telling him this morning if she would marry him, and he was probably scared that she might say yes.

She took her letters with her when she went downstairs. Some of the doors were open now, but she saw no sign of life until she reached the kitchen where Elena was washing up plates and glasses from the *festa*.

Elena smiled and said good morning, and left the sink to pour a cup of coffee from a pot on the hob of the stove.

'Thank you,' said Harriet. 'Where is everybody?'

'Up at the temple. They will be back soon.' They were helping in the clearing up, of course, and Harriet should have been giving them a hand.

'I overslept,' she apologised.

'The Signore said to let you sleep.' Jotham had known what time she came in last night, but he hadn't known that she didn't get to bed till dawn.

'Very hospitable of him,' Harriet said tartly.

'He is in the office,' Elena elaborated. 'When you came down he said he wished to see you.'

Harriet gulped some more coffee. It was hot and strong and it made her eyes water. 'Why not?' she said. She put down the half empty cup beside her letters, and walked across the hall into the *salotto*. There could be several reasons why her company was being requested. It could be a follow-on from yesterday, with Jotham still showing Nigel that Harriet enjoyed being with him. He could have waited for her, to walk up with her to join the party in the courtyard. It was unlikely he knew things had changed and Harriet would quite enjoy passing on the news that Nigel had asked her to marry him.

Jotham had tricked her, pretending to like her, making her like him. Because yesterday she had liked him. She had thought of him as a friend, the clasped hands, the trust, all the malarky. It rankled, so that when she rapped on the office door both her hands were clenched into fists. 'Come in,' he called.

He was behind the desk and papers were all over it. He glanced up, said, 'Hello, sit down, will you?' and went on writing. Just like the last time. What happened if he broke off in the middle of a page or a sentence? she wondered. Was his train of thought shattered for hours, or did he just do it to get the advantage by making the intruder wait?

She opened her mouth to say, 'Call me when you're through,' then she would have walked out of the room; but he looked up suddenly and asked,

'What's this about Nigel asking you to marry him?' and that left her gasping.

It astonished her that Nigel had told Jotham, especially as Harriet hadn't given her answer. She would have expected Nigel to be the one leaving messages about seeing her, unless of course he had reconsidered and left Joth to explain that his marriage proposal was a slip of the tongue.

The way Jotham Gaul carried on as spokesman for the Joliffe family that wouldn't be so surprising.

'Well?' said Joth.

'Exactly,' said Harriet. 'Well?'

'He did, I suppose? He wasn't drunk or dreaming?'

'He wasn't drunk. I don't think he was dreaming.' Curiosity made her ask, 'What did he tell you?'

'That he asked you to marry him last night, and you're thinking it over.'

She wondered if he had heard the door next to his open and close, and seen Nigel leave her room. She doubted if the information had been volunteered, but she knew that once Jotham started cross-examining Nigel would talk.

Not me, she thought. You'll get nothing out of me that I don't want to tell, and she looked at the granite-like face and the piercing eyes and asked herself how she could ever have imagined this man was her friend.

'That's it,' she said, 'that's what happened,' and the corners of her closed lips curved upwards in a small malicious smile.

'You can stop looking like the cat with the cream,' he growled, 'because it is not on.'

He was angry, and getting angrier, and she wanted him to stop growling and start shouting, to jump up and bang the desk and send the papers flying, because that would be more satisfying than screaming her own head off.

She said, almost purring, 'I am the one to say whether it's on or not. You're out of the game now, even if you and his mother do think it will be the absolute end for Nigel if he gets himself landed with me. And that *festa* move, choosing me as your partner, wasn't so smart either. He got so worked up about what might have been going on when we were all alone on the hillside that he ended up proposing, so thanks a lot, partner.'

Jotham sat very still and he said very quietly, 'You are going to let him off the hook,' as though she had trapped the man and had him wriggling. To admit, right now, that she wasn't marrying Nigel would be like taking orders from Joth, and she said crisply.

'I'm going to marry him and you can't do a thing about it.'

He stood up, hooded eyes on her, face expressionless, and it was like his description of before a storm: everything deathly still and no air, so that you were gasping, choking, and you still couldn't breathe. He came round the desk, never taking his eyes off her, and when his outstretched hands reached for her she thought in terror—he could crush me. If he touches my throat or my head I must scream; but her throat was dryer than dust.

He put his hands on her shoulders, lightly, but she felt their weight. 'Now you tell me why you want to marry him,' he said.

'I've already told you. I want a part-share in Tudor House. As you say Sylvia Joliffe doesn't appreciate my sense of humour, there isn't much about me she does appreciate, but she'll have to try, won't she, when I'm her daughter-in-law?'

She must be out of her mind. Wasn't he angry enough? He wasn't going to hit the desk with his hands on her. He was more likely to hit her, or send her spinning across the room. But instead he took his hands away, and his mouth could have been starting a smile if his eyes hadn't stayed hard as flint.

'I certainly hope you've got other reasons,' he said.

She couldn't say, 'I love him.' She was lying already, pretending she was going to marry Nigel, but somehow she couldn't get that lie out. She shrugged and grimaced slightly, and Jotham's grin widened like the smile on the face of the tiger.

'If you haven't, Beauty,' he said, 'you're going to need your sense of humour.' She started and he told her, slowly as though he was enjoying this, 'Because I bought Tudor House from Nigel four years ago, just after his father died, although it isn't common knowledge. So if owning the house is your only reason for wanting to be Mrs Joliffe you'd better run along and say no, nicely.'

He had everything. Wherever she looked it seemed to be his: the factory, the Villa, now Tudor House, and she heard her voice, poisonous and sweet. 'It's fascinating to meet the man who has everything. Except a father, I'm told. Pity he didn't keep in touch. It would have been worth his while.'

That appalled her as she heard it, and at once she began to stammer, 'I'm sorry, I didn't mean——'

'Don't spoil it.' He was still grinning and he still looked like a tiger. 'That was a grand exit line. Damned if I can think of anything to cap it.'

She was outside the room, the door closed behind her, and she must have walked out because he hadn't touched her. She turned to open the door again and go back and say, 'I don't know what got into me. That was unforgivable. I don't know why I said it.' But he wouldn't be listening to anything else she said for a while, so she turned away from the door and went up the wide staircase to her room.

She felt punch-drunk, as though someone had been hitting her about the head, leaving her sick and muzzy. She had come to fetch her sunglasses. She hadn't worn them since she came here, but this morning she needed to hide behind a mask before she set off for the courtyard, to join the others. She wasn't anxious to face anybody, but if she went off on her own she would start thinking, about what had just happened, and that would only make her even more miserable.

She took the path through the olive groves, looking around, telling herself what a beautiful day it was, what a super holiday spot. But there was a limit to her capacity for shutting out the unpleasant thoughts.

She couldn't understand why she had been so suicidally bent on antagonising Joth. He was annoyed that Nigel had asked her to marry him—he was sure that Annie was the girl for Nigel and of course he was right—but Harriet had gone out of her way to fan that annoyance into violent anger.

She had been so upset herself that she had hardly known what she was saying. She had been in one of those outrageous childish rages when she had wanted to bring down the whole world, because those whom she loved didn't love her.

Didn't love her? Of course he didn't love her. Not Joth. He didn't even like her. But she liked him, of course she did. She stood stock still as understanding came to her. Yesterday had been so special because she had been falling in love, and that had never happened to her like this before with any man.

When she thought of Joth now she was seized with an immense longing to run back and throw herself into his arms, and let him hold her and love her and comfort her. But he wouldn't, and she couldn't go running to him, and she stood on the dry crumbling earth, beneath the olive trees and the burning sun, aching with loneliness, because she wanted him more than anything in the world and he would never want her at all.

CHAPTER NINE

HARRIET walked on towards the courtyard, from which thin ribbons of smoke were rising. She could hear the voices and she wanted to be where there were people—the more the better—but her feet dragged and depression closed over her like a grey shadow.

Joth had had no time for her from their first meeting, and even if he was begining to like her a little better what had just happened must have sent his opinion of her back to rock bottom. What a show of uncaring greed she had put on, and when she told Nigel she couldn't marry him Joth would probably believe it was because of Tudor House. She couldn't win. There must be something self-destructive in her. She must be the biggest fool breathing, and she was probably the unhappiest.

She was glad she had worn her sunglasses. Behind them her eyes were desperate, but she managed to stretch her lips into a smile as she came into the clearing and walked across to the courtyard.

There was a small bonfire right in the centre, in which the islanders were burning the dead flowers and greenery as well as the litter of papers and left-overs. Everything was going up in smoke and soon there would only be a pile of grey ash, which would scatter and vanish for ever.

I might have saved a leaf, Harriet thought, or taken a flower and pressed it. Or perhaps it was better that the wind should blow it all away. She wouldn't need souvenirs. She wanted to forget, not remember. She wanted Joth, and she could think of no way she would ever manage to forget him.

Nigel came to meet her, smiling, and hurrying to stop her before she reached the group where Erica and Alistair and Annie were unravelling creepers from a pillar. He caught her at the edge of the courtyard and said, 'Good morning, darling, you look beautiful.'

'Thank you,' she said mechanically.

'Have you thought about it?'

Marriage he meant, and he sounded anxious. But whether that was because he was hoping she'd say yes or no she wasn't sure. She doubted if he really knew himself. He wanted to stand here and talk about it, but she went on walking, slowly. 'I have thought about it,' she said, 'and I think we'd better forget last night, and just let things go on as they were.'

She wished last night could be wiped out, from when she had walked into her room and found Nigel waiting; and she wished this morning could. She wished it was yesterday. The way she felt right now she wished she was dead.

'I meant what I said.' Nigel was doggedly keeping step with her. 'I want to marry you.'

Annie was watching them. She had a strand of creeper in her hands and she was twisting it. Harriet caught her eyes and Annie turned away and Harriet thought, She's probably wishing she could strangle me.

She had never felt much sympathy for other girls' love problems before, but now the way that Annie felt echoed in her own heart. She hated the women in Joth's life. All of them, past, present and future. She knew that she would lie awake at nights, aching with longing, because she wanted to be the lover in his arms and some other woman was in her place.

'But there's something I must tell you,' Nigel was saying. 'About the house.' Harriet could have said, 'I know,' but it was less effort to let him go on. 'It belongs to Joth.

We needed the cash after my father died to keep the farm going. The farm's still mine, but the house is Joth's.'

'I see,' she murmured as he paused for a moment.

'Only I'd rather you didn't mention it to anyone.' They were still walking and Nigel put his head confidentially close. 'My mother, you know, it's always been her home ever since she got married, and as far as Joth's concerned she's still mistress of the place.'

Harriet had to smile, although she hid it quickly. So Sylvia Joliffe preferred to keep the neighbours in ignorance of the fact that she and Nigel were the tenants in Tudor House, not Jotham Gaul. And why not? That little bit of snobbish subterfuge did no harm, so far as Harriet could see. It was no one else's business anyway. She said, 'In a manner of speaking it's still in the family, isn't it?'

Nigel nodded. 'Joth, you mean? Yes, that's what he says.'

He could be wonderfully kind, but Harriet daren't think about that or she might have burst into tears, and she could just imagine herself sobbing, 'I want him to be kind to me. I want to stand right here, now, and howl for him.'

'But the farm's mine,' Nigel repeated. 'And we'd live in the house. You always said you loved the house.'

Because she had wanted something strong and secure around her, but all she wanted now were Joth's arms. She said, 'Let's leave it shall we? Let's wait and see,' and she went to the bonfire and picked up some of the limp dried-out leaves from the pile and fed them into the flames.

'I had to tell Joth.' Nigel followed her to tell her that. 'I think he knew I'd seen you last night after you came in. There isn't much gets by him.' He threw on a few leaves himself. 'There isn't anything,' he said. 'Anyhow, I told him I'd asked you to marry me and you'd said you'd think about it.'

Harriet didn't enquire if the others knew. Nobody said

they did. Annie smiled her subdued little smile when she said, 'Hello,' and Alistair and Erica grinned knowingly. But that turned out to be because Harriet hadn't been home by midnight, and neither had Joth.

'Where did you two get to last night?' Erica hissed, as soon as she managed a quiet word with Harriet. 'Nigel was like a cat on hot bricks all evening.'

'We went climbing.' Harriet looked up, and she could see the spot they had reached, the great mass of the volcano rising above it.

'No wonder you overslept this morning,' Erica leered wickedly.

'I fell asleep up there' said Harriet. 'We got a fair way up and then we sat down and I fell asleep. I slept for hours.'

'And Joth let you?' Erica squeaked, her eyebrows going up and down in comical astonishment. 'That doesn't sound much like Joth to me. Not that I'd know,' she added wistfully, 'but from what I hear.'

At the time Harriet had thought he was more considerate than any other man she had ever known, but perhaps it would have created problems if he had woken her and made love to her. Perhaps he didn't want to get involved. She said, 'Perhaps he fell asleep too. It was a long day.'

She worked hard, helping to clear the courtyard. It was swelteringly hot, but she kept going, although the sweat was pouring off her. She had kept going yesterday, but then there had been the buffet; and wine and fruit drinks cool from the dark cave of the temple. She had been strong and gay and happy yesterday. Today she kept moving because she didn't want to sit around, talking seriously with anybody, and because she must be dead beat when she went to bed tonight.

Otherwise she would be pacing the room again, or tossing and turning on her bed all night, with the little balcony outside and Joth's window open.

He'd turned up a few minutes after Harriet—while she was still standing by the bonfire with Nigel, before they joined the others—and he'd walked across and asked cheerfully, 'Still considering the offer, are you? Still giving it your earnest attention?'

Nigel looked embarrassed, there was mockery in Joth's bonhomie, and Harriet begged, 'Please shut up!'

'I'll give you ten to one she won't marry you,' said Joth, and Harriet hurled her handful of crumpled papers into the middle of the fire and went striding off to join the others.

She knew she was amusing Joth with all this rushing about. He was watching her, and when he saw her looking at him he grinned back. He didn't believe there was any risk now that she might marry Nigel. If it hadn't been for Sylvia wanting to keep it a secret, that the Joliffes no longer owned Tudor House, he would probably have told her that at the beginning.

He thought that settled it, and now she was working off temper and tantrums. He had called her 'a spoiled child', that was how he had always considered her, and it was too late to start acting grave and sensible for the rest of the holiday.

She couldn't have done it anyway. It wasn't her nature, and the restlessness was on her, worse than ever.

After lunch, when they went down to the beach, she dropped her towel and sunglasses on the sand and turned to Joth. 'Race you?' she said.

Her one-piece suit was the colour of her skin, she was like a slim gilt figurine poised at the water's edge, and almost any man would have looked admiringly at her, but Joth seemed unimpressed. 'Why?' he said, and she tossed back her mane of hair.

'To prove I can swim faster.' He was still wearing slacks,

and a shirt open to the waist, but they had come down to the beach to swim, so he would have trunks on. She fixed him with glinting provocative eyes, and he grinned and drawled,

'Can you hell as like.' He had brought a black leather folder with him. Now he sat down on a rock and opened it and took out some papers, bulldog-clipped together, and Harriet commented,

'You never let up, do you?'

'Not often,' he agreed, and she wanted to plead, 'Please come. Let's swim right out and leave them all behind.' But everybody was listening, and Joth wouldn't have taken a couple of steps with her because she asked him to, although yesterday they had walked hand in hand. She had to get into the water where it wouldn't matter if the mist in her eyes was tears.

'You want to race?' said Nigel. Last time it had been Erica's challenge, and Harriet had trailed behind them all. This time she said,

'Sure,' and ran into the sea and struck out for the rock, cleaving through the water at such speed that when she pulled herself up on to the flat-topped rock not one of them was near.

She sat, knees under her chin, hands clasped round her ankles, smiling at the astonished faces swimming towards her. Alistair touched the rock first, blowing out a mouthful of water and gasping, 'You might have mentioned you were a gold medallist!'

'I like swimming,' she said. 'It's one of the few things I do well.'

She dived off again, as Nigel and Annie and Erica reached the rock, and swam out into the open sea, away from them all. Maybe she could live in the water for the rest of the holiday, looking for dolphins, coming up for food and air. The water caressed her from head to foot, rippling along her skin like the lightest of kisses, and she dived deep until her lungs were bursting and there was a roaring in her ears. Then she floated up again into the bright light.

Nigel was standing on the rock. As her head bobbed up he cupped his mouth to make his voice carry and shouted, 'Harriet, you're too far out!'

'How would you know?' she muttered. 'I'm all right!' she called back. 'It's wonderful, I'm having the time of my life!'

This holiday could be her last chance for this kind of swimming for a long time, because she would be starting work in the Gallery as soon as she got home, which would be something of a surprise to most of her friends. Anthony for one. He would be pleased to see her again, and she tried to tell herself she was looking forward to seeing him.

She was, in a vague sort of way, but the thought of Joth pushed all other men out of her mind. She was searching for him now, wondering if he might swim after her if she stayed out here long enough. But he'd been fooled once by her cries for help, he'd know she wasn't in difficulties.

She bobbed high and she could see him still on the beach. He wasn't coming out, she was nowhere in his mind, and it was hopeless wondering if they might meet again in England, to a fresh start. There was no chance for her with Joth. If there had been she must have killed it stone dead this morning. How could she have said that about his father? How could anyone say anything as savage and insensitive as that?

'I'm sorry,' she whispered, 'I'm sorry, I'm sorry.'

Someone was swimming towards her—Nigel, and she sighed and set off to meet him. 'You're getting too far out,' he protested again as they reached each other.

'Why? I'm not going to get run down by a fishing boat, am I?'

'The swimming's just as good in the bay.'

'Not for me,' she said. 'I like the wide open spaces.' She was being rotten to Nigel, but at least she could do this for him and Annie before the holiday ended, show Nigel that his infatuation for herself had never been more than skin deep.

She left him behind and swam to the jetty steps and ran, with the sun throwing a black shadow at her heels, along the jetty and up on to the rocks. By the time Nigel was coming out of the water Harriet was on the edge of the overhanging cliff shelf.

There was no one swimming beneath her, but they were all looking up, from the rocks, from the beach, and she blew kisses, showing off, again like a badly brought up child. Nigel shouted 'Harriet!' as she went into a swallow dive like a bird.

This was fantastic. She could do this all day long. So long as the tide was in, of course. She broke surface and got a hoorah from Alistair, still sunning himself on the flat-topped rock. Annie and Erica were in the shallows, and as Harriet waded up to them Erica exclaimed 'Wow!' and Annie muttered,

'Aren't you scared of anything?'

'Of course I am.' Of loneliness and growing old, and loving a man who didn't love you and being terrified that the hurt would last and last until you were old. 'But not of diving,' said Harriet.

Joth still sat where she had left him, leather folder at his feet and the papers in his hand. Nigel was pacing up and down at the sea's edge, irritated with himself for getting panicky and yelling, annoyed with Harriet. He greeted her with, 'What was that in aid of?'

'I felt like taking a high dive,' she said airily, and she

padded up to the towels and retrieved hers and began to rub her hair. Nigel followed, tight-lipped, demanding querulously,

'Do you have to make an exhibition of everything you do?'

She paused in her towelling to consider, then nodded, 'Yes, I suppose I do.'

'You want to marry the girl and you don't know that?' Joth's deep voice rumbled with amusement and Nigel muttered,

'Well, it's bloody crazy, diving from up there. I don't care how good a swimmer you are.'

'She drives cars too fast too,' said Joth.

'Don't you care?' cried Nigel. 'Suppose you had an accident, suppose you ended up disfigured?'

Her face was in the towel and her voice was muffled. 'Then I'd find out who my real friends were,' she said, and she shivered in the hot sun.

The days went by and the holiday should have been wonderful. They spent hours on the beach, they went day-long cruises in a hired sixteen-foot high-prowed boat, and out with the fishing fleet during one star-studded night. They crossed to the mainland for shopping trips, eating in cafés in the square, and explored the island, keeping to the lower slopes of the volcano.

Harriet hurled herself into every expedition, every experience. She insisted on trying out the fishing bucket seat in the stern of the hired boat, hooked a fish large enough to bend the rod, and stood up and tried to reel it in herself, screaming at everyone else to keep back until she was yanked overboard. They had to turn about to fish her out, unrepentant and laughing about the one that got away.

She wanted to climb to the rim of the volcano. She suggested it several times, but she got no takers to accom-

pany her, and when she said, 'I'll go up on my own, then,'
Joth said,

'Not while I'm here you won't.' He didn't say he'd do
the climb with her, he just said she wouldn't, and she
pulled a face indicating who-does-he-think-he's-bossing-
around, but she knew that he'd stop her all right if she
tried to.

The streak of wildness in Harriet, that had enchanted
Nigel at the begining, was starting to get him down, as
she meant it to. He would always be fascinated by her but
he couldn't see himself keeping up with her pace for a
lifetime. Perhaps it was as well that he didn't own Tudor
House, because without it he didn't have much to offer
a girl like Harriet. And he was beginning to be glad that
Annie had insisted on coming along, because a man knew
where he was with a girl like Annie.

They were all having a splendid holiday, and Harriet
seemed to be enjoying every minute of it. Nobody sus-
pected that she was longing for it to end. The days were
filled with sunshine and laughter, rushing around, cram-
ming in as much as she could, while Joth smiled and let
her get on with it.

If she wanted to swim away from the others, or rock
climb when there was an easy path, that was her look-
out. Very rarely he said no, like going up to the rim of
the volcano. But most of the time he treated her as an
amusingly tiresome child. Not his child—somebody else's.
Not his responsibility unless she looked like getting completely out of hand. Nothing she did was likely to bother
Joth, although at least some of this hyper-activity was to
keep him noticing her.

She made sure that she was tired by night, and most
nights she slept quite well, but if she should wake in the
middle hours she would lie in the darkness going over
and over the same waking dream. That she went out on

to the balcony and called through Joth's window and he came out and they talked.

She imagined in so many ways the words that would tell him how lonely she was, how much she needed and wanted him. She tried not to go beyond words, because when she thought of him touching her her body would react with an explosion of desire, convulsing her with a raging, agonising hunger, and there would be no more sleep for her for hours.

In fact she knew that she would never dare go out on to the balcony because there would be no welcome for her from the man who was sleeping in the next room. Joth would soon pack her off to her own bed, and that would hurt worse than any other rejection of her whole life. She didn't want that among her memories when she got away from here.

Of course it would be better once she was away. When she wasn't spending her days with him the nights would be easier. She would get through this holiday and then she would start a new life and a new job, and Jotham Gaul would have no part in either ...

But on the Wednesday of the second—and last—week of the holiday she came down to breakfast and Joth had gone. The others were around the kitchen table, eating their croissants, and it was Alistair who said something about 'when Joth gets back.'

Harriet looked up from the warm roll she was breaking to ask, 'What do you mean, gets back? Where's he gone?'

Business had taken him to the mainland, and a helicopter to a meeting in Naples. Everybody but Harriet knew that his schedule had included this trip, and it should have been a relief to her. It would mean that she could relax for a couple of days, and for two nights the room next to hers would be mercifully empty. But her immediate reaction was a let-down, as sudden as though she had fallen into a black hole. Everything inside and around her went heavy as lead, dull, flat, no life and no sparkle left.

She was in love with a man who wouldn't have her as a gift. While he was around she was perpetually on edge, spurred to all sorts of outrageous behaviour just to keep him looking her way, but when he wasn't here there was nothing.

That was how it felt. Because Joth wasn't sitting at this table, or in his office just across the hall, the warm new bread had no taste and the day stretching ahead was empty. In a brief flash Harriet knew what life would be without him, and it was like a foretaste of death.

Erica, sitting beside her, said anxiously, 'Are you all right? You've gone awfully pale.'

The golden tan of Harriet's skin was the colour of old ivory, and then they were all concerned, all hovering around her. Nobody associated it with the fact that Joth would be away for a couple of days, but they all pointed out that she had been overdoing things, rushing around in this heat. She admitted to a headache, and Annie brought her some pills, and the colour came back to her face.

But there was no colour in the day. It was drab from morning till night, although she managed to fool them all. She was enjoying nothing without Joth, and now her plans had undergone a complete change.

When they got back they must keep in touch. That wouldn't be difficult, there was the factory, mutual friends; she'd make sure they met, and when he saw her working hard for a living he'd realise she wasn't a spoiled child.

Before they left here she would apologise for what she'd said the morning after the *festa*, explain that she was upset and confused, and that she'd known she wasn't right for Nigel. Although she'd said she was going to marry him she had never meant it, not for a moment.

That night, in her room, she rehearsed what she would say. Her only chance of getting Joth really alone was at night; and if she went to his window and said, 'Please, I have to talk to you,' then surely he would come out on to the balcony and listen to her.

The second night she went out on the balcony, his room empty behind her. She closed her eyes and held on to the rail, feeling the silver moonlight on her blind face, and whispered, 'Please, I'm sorry ...' When she had said it all she rubbed her shoulder. Her skin felt clammily cold and she thought—surely he will put his hand on my shoulder. Any friend would do that after an apology. Surely he will touch me and say it's all right.

And the need for his touch spread through every fibre of her body so that scalding tears slid down her face, but weeping brought no relief ...

It was late next day when Joth came back. They were all sitting on the verandah, drinking thick sweet coffee in tiny cups and brandy in balloon glasses, although Harriet had hardly touched her brandy. She wanted to keep a cool head because if she was the least bit muzzy she just might tell Joth how badly she'd missed him, in front of them all, and that would be wearing her heart on her sleeve with a vengeance.

As soon as they spotted the lights of the little boat, out beyond the bay, they hurried down to the jetty and waited for it to moor alongside. 'Good trip?' Nigel shouted, and Joth waved from the prow of the boat,

'It's in the bag, boyo.'

'What's in the bag?' asked Annie.

'The business deal,' said Alistair. 'Whatever it was.'

I wish he'd come back a loser for once, thought Harriet, because when I say, 'Please let's be friends,' tonight I shall be talking to the tycoon who can't go wrong. I wish there was some way of making him believe that I would feel exactly the same if he had nothing at all.

As Joth stepped on to the jetty Annie and Erica ran to him, and he hugged the pair of them. 'We've missed you,' said Annie.

'And I've missed all of you,' said Joth.

I couldn't say that laughing, thought Harriet, and if he put his arms around me I could go up in flames.

As they started to walk along the jetty, towards the steps leading up to the lights of the villa, Joth turned to her and asked, 'You haven't been climbing up the volcano?'

From down on the beach it seemed so high that the stars hung in clusters around it. 'No,' she said, then she had a brilliant idea. 'Hey, I never did get my forfeit from the *festa*. Weren't you supposed to give me anything I asked for? How about taking me up there then?'

He laughed. 'All right. Tomorrow.'

There were hoots of derision from the rest. Who wanted to spend their last day scrambling up pumice slopes? It would be hot, dusty, horrible. They were having a picnic in the afternoon and relaxing. Next day the journey home started. Why on earth should Harriet want to go volcano climbing in a temperature that would fry eggs?

She wanted to go because no one but Joth was likely to come, and it would be easier to talk up there. She would have time. She could bring the conversation casually round to her apology, without making such a drama of it.

Now that Joth was here, and night was on them, she honestly didn't think she had the nerve to go to his room and blurt out the confession she had rehearsed. At the thought of it she was overwhelmed with a shyness she had never known before.

The picnic was an extra special one. Elena had filled a huge hamper with delicacies and fruit, and they spread a white linen cloth under the trees and ate their last alfresco meal on Picola Licata, washing it down with the sweet local wines.

'You're not serious about going up there are you?' Erica asked Harriet, when some of the heat of the day had abated, and Harriet said quickly

'Of course I am.'

'You'll never make it' said Annie; and she probably wouldn't, it was a tough climb. But at least she could show Joth that she didn't give up when the going got hard. He respected the fighters, and getting to the rim of the volcano was a challenge.

'Ready when you are' he said. She jumped to her feet, brushing crumbs from her skirt, tying a cotton scarf over her head, the knot at the back, under her hair.

'When do we send out the search party?' asked Nigel and Joth said,

'You don't. We'll be back.'

'So don't wait up for us,' Harriet quipped, and bit her lip. It was a flip remark, spoken without thought, but their laughter brought a return of that shyness that made her wonder whether she would ever be able to tell Joth anythink about how she felt.

I'll climb first she thought. I'll get as high as I can. If I get to the top I'll feel marvellous because I'll have made it, and then I can say, 'That's one obstacle scaled, now there's another, I want to apologise . . .'

She went at the climb with single-minded determination. There were no sheer surfaces but the rise was steep and steady, and once they were through the circle of cultivated land they met the rock. They had exchanged a few remarks at first, mostly about the building that would be done here sometime, but then Joth said, 'From now on I'd advise you to save your breath.'

She nodded, a little breathless already. The surface of the

volcano was arid and bare, except for small plants that filled the crevices where water was held, and the soles of her feet burned through her shoes from heat reflected back from the rock.

It was a hellish climb, and after about an hour of it she knew that Joth was waiting for her to admit she had had enough. He looked as hot as she was but he wasn't breathless, and she took his hand over the crumbling rocks and the spearheads of lava, and it became a battle with herself to get to the top because she might never be three-quarters up a volcano again.

At first he had walked with her, helped her, humoured her, but after the three-quarter mark he was in earnest about it, as though he knew that she would be bitterly disappointed if she didn't make it.

She gasped 'Thanks' when he said 'Hold it for a moment' and she leaned against him, getting her strength back. 'You'll do it,' he said. 'We're nearly there.'

Yes, she thought, I can do it. With you I could do anything. And she smiled and nodded because she daren't trust herself to speak.

From the rim they looked right down into the ash-covered bottom of the volcano, marbled here and there by hard black lava streams. The edges of the cone showed streaks of coloured rock—browns and reds and yellows and whites—through the pumice and the lava, and the precipitous walls were jagged. Only an experienced climber should venture down there and Harriet turned and Joth said, 'Yes I have and no you can't.'

'It never crossed my mind,' she said. 'Not today anyway.'

She didn't have the breath to talk, but he was smiling at her. Later she would tell him. I love you, she thought, I love you, I love you, and I'm scared to tell you, but

tonight I will make myself beautiful again and then it might
be easier.

She said, 'I must look like the end of the world.'

'You look fine. Shall we be getting back?'

She had a few bruises and a few cuts and grazes to show
for the climb up, but it was on the way down that she
put her foot on a thin crust of lava over a shallow crevice.
Joth grabbed her as she fell, but she landed with her cheek
against the rough rocks and felt a sharp cutting jab.

'This has got to stop,' he said, lifting her into a sitting
position. 'I can't stand much more of this.'

She knew she had been a nuisance all along, but it hurt
horribly hearing him say it. Worse than the smart of the
cut, and she looked at the small streak of blood on her
fingers as she took them from her cheek.

'It's all right,' he said. 'It's only a scratch, you're not disfigured.'

She smiled wanly. 'Nigel seems to think that would be
the very worst thing that could ever happen to me.'

'Would it?' he asked, and she answered with another
question,

'Do you think I'm beautiful?'

'Most of the time. Sometimes you can look an ugly
little tike.' But he sounded as though he found that rather
endearing, and he took a white handkerchief out of his
pocket and dabbed the cut on her cheek. 'All right?'

'Fine,' she said. 'Just fine.'

As they came carefully down the bare slopes Harriet said,
'Could we go back via the temple? I'd like to say goodbye to the temple.'

'Of course,' said Joth, and they moved across the rough
terrain, heading for the path they had climbed on the
night of the *festa*.

When we reach the temple, Harriet thought, I'll say,
'This was the best day of my life. Right until I walked

into my bedroom and found Nigel waiting it was the best day I ever had.'

They reached the little plantation of silver firs first and it was no use saying things in her head, she could go on for ever doing that. They had been talking about how the Villa would look when it was restored. She was describing the decor in an Italian palace she had once stayed in, when they came to the grassy slope where she had fallen asleep in Joth's arms and she said suddenly, 'I'm not marrying Nigel.'

'Of course you're not.' He wasn't surprised. Everybody knew that by now. But he did stop walking and turn to look at her.

She said, 'His mother will be pleased, won't she? He said you'd do anything for her.'

His eyebrows raised slightly. 'I would do a great deal. What have I done this time?'

Everything he planned to do, according to Nigel. She said, 'Picked me as your partner at the *festa*. Put a stop to it. Nigel and me,' and the grizzled eyebrows went higher.

'Well, I wasn't doing that for Sylvia. Nor for Nigel.'

'You mean for Annie?'

'You must think I'm a charitable institution. I do quite a lot of things for myself.'

Harriet heard her own soft gasp. 'But you told Nigel he'd be a fool to get himself landed with a girl like me.'

'So he would,' said Joth promptly, 'you'd never give him a moment's peace. But I'd be a much bigger fool if I didn't get myself landed with you.'

'You're joking!'

'Am I?' He wasn't smiling, so why hadn't he stopped her that morning. She wailed,

'Why didn't you just say 'Please don't marry him' the morning after the *festa*?'

'He said you were thinking it over. I'd thought there was an understanding between us and you could have told him no right away.'

'I said that to get him out of my room. "Thank you," I said, "I'll sleep on it, goodnight".'

Joth's lips twitched, although the grin was wry.

'That's simple enough. That didn't occur to me. I never realised that being jealous could make me stupid.'

The weakness seemed to be in her knees so that she had to sit down on the soft springy turf, and it was turning her voice into a croak. 'You didn't act jealous.'

'Of course I didn't, I'm good at the waiting game.' He sat down beside her. 'But if you and Nigel had been getting closer together instead of further apart I'd have played a different hand.'

'Like what?'

'Tudor House?' He shrugged, 'Well, you wanted it, didn't you?' Then he grinned, 'Seduction? And I'm damn sure I'm better at that than Nigel.'

'I'll bet you are,' murmured Harriet. She put her chin on his shoulder and he put an arm around her and asked, 'Did you miss me the last two days?'

'Yes, I did.'

'I couldn't get it out of my head that you'd be over the top of the volcano or swimming to the mainland if I didn't get back here to keep an eye on you.'

That was the kindest thing anyone had ever said to her, that they worried about her when she wasn't there. She said, 'I don't always carry on like this, you know.'

He raised her face from the hollow of his collarbone, with gentle fingers. 'I don't think you will,' he said, as though he knew that the restless days were over. 'But you need watching over.' He touched the cut on her cheek, lightly, and smiled. 'And I'm the man to watch out for you.'